The Devil's Disciple

The Devil's Disciple

Hamao Shirō

Translated by J. Keith Vincent

Hesperus Worldwide

Hesperus Worldwide
Published by Hesperus Press Limited
19 Bulstrode Street, London w1u 2jn
www.hesperuspress.com

'The Devil's Disciple' was first published in Japanese as 'Akuma no deshi'
in the April 1929 issue of *Shinseinen*.
'Did He Kill Them?' was first published in Japanese as 'Kare ga koroshita ka'
in the January and February 1929 issues of *Shinseinen*.

This collection first published by Hesperus Press, 2011
Introduction and English language translation © J. Keith Vincent, 2011

Designed and typeset by Fraser Muggeridge studio
Printed in the UK by CPI Mackays, Chatham

isbn: 978-1-84391-857-8

Contents

Note on Japanese Name Order

In this volume, Japanese names are given in the Japanese order, with the family name first followed by the given name. For example: 'Hamao Shirō'.

Introduction

Hamao Shirō's career as a writer of detective fiction lasted only six years before his tragically early death at the age of forty. During that time he produced sixteen novellas and three full-length novels, leaving a final one unfinished. The stories included here are the first two he ever published, both in 1929, in the pages of *New Youth*, a wildly popular magazine that promoted the heady brew of aestheticised decadence, gothic horror, and pseudo-scientific sexology and criminology known in 1920s Japan as *ero-guro-nansensu* or 'erotic grotesque nonsense'. Like most of the work written under this banner, these early stories have a *noir*-ish feel that some readers may find a little dated and, perhaps a lot, over the top. But they are still very much worth reading despite these flaws, I submit, for the window they offer into interwar Japan, for the provocative questions they pose about sexuality, justice and the law, and – last but not least – for a certain campy sensibility that is perhaps not surprising given that Hamao was also one of Japan's earliest apologists for male homosexuality.

Hamao Shirō (1896–1935) was born into one of modern Japan's most powerful families and married into another. His grandfather, Baron Katō Hiroyuki, was a conservative legal scholar who gave lectures to the Meiji Emperor and served twice as the President of Tokyo Imperial University. His father was Baron Katō Terumaro, a member of the House of Peers and a prominent physician in the service of both the Meiji and Taisho Emperors. In 1918 Shirō married the daughter of Viscount Hamao Arata, another past president of Tokyo Imperial University and a founder of the Tokyo School of Fine Arts. Upon Arata's death in 1925, Shirō, who had already taken the Hamao name, inherited the title of Viscount. It was also in this year that he was appointed as a public prosecutor in the Tokyo District Court at the young age of twenty-nine.

He did not remain a prosecutor for long, however. Within three years he had resigned his position, opened a private law practice, and begun a new career writing detective fiction. His society friends were no doubt aghast that he had given up this prestigious position in order to write in such a lowbrow genre, but Hamao had decided that rather than trying to follow in the footsteps of his grandfather, who had helped create the modern Japanese legal system, he would use his talents to write fiction that would critique it. His work as a prosecutor had served only to disillusion him with the workings of the law and to confirm the critical insider's perspective his upbringing had given him on the upper echelons of government and the legal profession. Detective fiction was a way to work through that disillusionment and to explore the fallibility of the law. At the same time, as the first detective novelist in Japan to have a law degree and experience as a prosecutor, he was able to bring a degree of legal expertise to his work that was sorely lacking in most detective fiction in Japan at the time. Both of the stories translated here deal with this theme of the law's fallibility, as does the only other story by Hamao published thus far in English, 'The Execution of Ten'ichibo', beautifully translated by Jeffrey Angles in volume 32, issue number 2, of *Critical Asian Studies* (2005).

Pre-war Japanese detective fiction typically fell into one of two categories. In the 'orthodox' (*honkaku*) variety the detective identifies the culprit through brilliant feats of reasoning and, by solving the mystery, repairs the damage the crime has done to the social fabric. In this variety the narrator tends to have a dependably objective and unbiased perspective and refrains from playing tricks on the reader. This relatively reassuring and socially conservative form was the norm in Japan beginning in the 1880s with the translation of authors like Arthur Conan Doyle and Émile Gaboriau. It was not until the 1920s, however, with the introduction of the 'heterodox', or *henkaku* style, that detective fiction really took off in Japan. In heterodox detective fiction, which traces its roots both to Edgar Allan Poe and to writers of 'pure' literature such as Tanizaki Jun'ichirō and Akutagawa Ryūnosuke, the narrators are not as reliable, and while the crime may be 'solved' the reader is far from reassured. While orthodox detective fiction tended to draw clear distinctions between guilt and innocence, good and evil, in the heterodox form these lines became deliciously blurred.

Hamao's work encompassed both orthodox and heterodox elements. In his longer works, such as *Satsujinki* (*The Murderer*), 1932, which was loosely based on S.S. Van Dine's 1928 novel *The Greene Murder Case*, the emphasis was on 'whodunit'. As in Van Dine's novel, the plot of *The Murderer* was so tightly constructed and the culprit so brilliantly concealed that Hamao's friend and fellow detective novelist Edogawa Ranpo praised it as a model of the orthodox form. And yet even in this most orthodox of his novels, Hamao showed heterodox tendencies that distinguished his work from that of Van Dine. Whereas Van Dine's detective Phylo Vance was a Holmes-like figure, preternaturally clever and pedantic, Hamao's detective Fujieda Shintarō relied on emotional intelligence and intuition.

In the two novellas translated here, Hamao clearly prefers the blurrier ground of the heterodox. There is no detective protagonist in either, nor is the focus precisely on the 'solving' of a crime. Questions of guilt or innocence matter less than the exploration of psychologically complex motives. In 'The Devil's Disciple' the narrator is an accused murderer writing a letter to his ex-lover who happens to be a prosecutor in the court where he is being tried. While he insists on his innocence of the crime he is accused of, his narrative is motivated less by a desire to prove it in a court of law than to blame the prosecutor for everything that has gone wrong in his life. In the process, he projects what seems to be his own homophobia and misogyny onto his former lover and also onto the legal system that he represents. In 'Did He Kill Them?' the narrative takes the form of a speech given by its barrister narrator to an audience of detective novelists, a conceit that allows Hamao to explore on a meta-fictional level the differences between his own brand of detective fiction and that practised by the orthodox school. In both stories scepticism about the law is delivered with an equal dose of scepticism about the reliability of narrators. In 'The Devil's Disciple' the narrator's obsessive, homophobic rancour toward the prosecutor makes it impossible to know how far to trust what he says, and the story offers us no external perspective from which to judge. In 'Did He Kill Them?' the narrator lacks the paranoid intensity of 'The Devil's Disciple' but the story still plays with the effects of (homo)sexual attraction on legal and narratorial objectivity.

When the narrator of 'Did He Kill Them?' states matter-of-factly that he is 'a man who is quite capable of appreciating a good-looking youth', he is probably expressing the author's tastes as well. Hamao had a scholarly and perhaps also a personal interest in male homosexuality that makes itself known in more or less subtle ways in most of his work. Ranpo called him 'my teacher on the subject of homosexuality' and, like the prosecutor Tsuchida in 'The Devil's Disciple', he was well versed in the work of European homophiles and radical sexologists such as Edward Carpenter, Karl-Heinrich Ulrichs, Magnus Hirschfeld, and Havelock Ellis. While sex and love between men was widely accepted and even celebrated in pre-modern Japan, by the 1930s modern sexology and psychiatry had recast it as a pathology and a perversion. Hamao was one of the first writers to oppose this. In 1930 he published an essay in a women's magazine in which he argued that homosexuality was not an illness but an innate aspect of personality. After the article came out he received a flood of letters from closeted 'urnings' (Ulrichs' term for men loving men) all over Japan who described the pressure their families put on them to marry, their sense of shame about their homosexuality and their fear that it should be revealed. In response to these letters Hamao wrote another article in the same magazine addressed to all of Japan's 'urnings' in which he encouraged them not to be ashamed and called for a greater understanding and tolerance. With this letter Hamao became one of Japan's first modern advocates for what would later be called 'gay rights'. While in this sense Hamao was very much ahead of his time, it is worth noting that his attitude had as much to do with his access to a cultural memory of a less homophobic past as it did with his anticipation of a more liberated future. One of the most fascinating aspects of 'The Devil's Disciple' is the way it captures a moment of historical overlap between two different 'regimes' of sexuality by giving us a nostalgic view of a still normative schoolboy homosexuality in the past seen through the lens of an increasingly paranoid and homophobic present.

Note

As the reader will soon discover, the game of mahjong plays an important role in 'Did He Kill Them?'. Hamao himself was a great fan of the game. He served as president of the Tokyo Mahjong Society and even had a special room reserved for mahjong in his house. For these reasons it was crucial to achieve an accurate translation of the mahjong game and, not being a player myself, I was very grateful for the help of my friend Kitamaru Yūji in the translation of those passages. I would also like to thank Martha Pooley of Hesperus Press for her infinite patience and brilliant editing.

The Devil's Disciple

I

Mr Tsuchida Hachirō, Esq.
Prosecuting Barrister at the XX District Court

I, Shimaura Eizō, a prisoner awaiting trial, have taken the liberty of sending this letter to you, Prosecutor Tsuchida, my erstwhile friend who was once more dear to me than a brother.

You do remember me, don't you Mr Prosecutor? My case may have been investigated by another prosecutor and landed on the desk of another judge, but as the accused in the sensational murder of a beautiful woman, no doubt my name has been all over the newspapers. Since you work in the same court in which I am being tried you could hardly have failed to notice my name in connection with this case. You must have heard of it.

If you had agreed to meet me I might have been spared the writing of this letter. If I had remembered earlier that my old friend was serving in the court attached to the very prison in which I am being held, I might not have had to suffer as long as I have. I might have been able much earlier to relate the bizarre experiences that I am about to set down here.

Prosecutor Tsuchida, I am being held here as a murderer. But the truth is that I am probably not that murderer. That's right. *Probably*. It saddens me to have to say this. And I apologise for expressing it in such an odd way. But if you will be so kind as to read this letter through to the end I promise that you will understand.

The horrific things I am about to describe are not entirely without relation to you. In fact it is fair to say that it is you who have made me suffer so. And because of that only you can understand my pain. Part of me hates you for this. I curse you for it. But now I beg you. I bow down before you. In the name of that friendship we once shared, that friendship of unparalleled closeness, I beg of you to believe what I have to say.

II

Let me address you as Tsuchida-san.

I shouldn't think that would be a problem.

Tsuchida-san, I ask you for a moment to step aside from your imposing profession as a prosecutor and think back to how things were a decade ago. Think back to our student days, when we had just put secondary school behind us and passed the next hurdle to those tearful, torrid days when we lived in the school dormitories.

We were best friends. Actually we were even more than best friends were we not? Was I not always to be seen at your side wherever you were and you at mine, no matter where we went? Were we not known among our dormitory mates as a *Paar*?

You are three years older than I am. You were the older brother looking for a younger one. I was young – still a child really – and I was overawed by the strength of your personality. Soon I had become your one-and-only little brother. Surely you cannot have forgotten this.

I thought I had found someone who could understand my loneliness. Even better, you were kind enough to love me. On top of that, you were brilliant. I respected you and came to believe that you could do no wrong.

For two years our friendship burned like a flame. The opposite sex was nothing to us. After those two years you graduated and went on to a top university. And what happened to us?

We split up all of a sudden. All too suddenly. And after that we barely saw each other again. Tsuchida-san, you, of course, were the cause of our break-up. You left me because you fell passionately in love with a beautiful boy one year below me in school.

Did you ever deign to ask yourself how your younger brother felt after you so carelessly tossed him aside out of fickleness?

I thought we loved and understood each other. I thought our friendship would last forever. But you stopped caring and left me all alone. I looked hard at myself from within that loneliness. I saw myself quite clearly there, and the self that I saw had no choice but to revile and curse you.

Self-absorbed as you are, you will no doubt interpret whatever I say to your own advantage.

Your face will contort into that devilish smile of yours as you picture to yourself a woman abandoned by her lover and despising him for his cruelty. But that's not what was going on at all. I had other reasons to hate you.

So yes, we were lovers of a sort. And I was forsaken by my lover. But getting away from you allowed me to take a good look at myself and at you as well, all the way through you.

Tsuchida-san. You are the most dangerous person in this world.

You are a devil. Devouring the flesh of humans is not enough for you. You are a hateful devil who won't stop until you have cast their very souls into hell.

You were a brilliant prodigy. You had an intellect of rare penetration. (And I suspect you still do.) But with that brain and that eloquence what did you do to the young men who gravitated toward you? What did you teach them? Have you, at least in my case, ever given a thought to how you warped their personalities?

You spoke with passion and preached with tears. The most irrational ideas sounded rational on your lips. The most specious rhetoric sounded utterly logical when it came from you. But what was it all in the end? Did it not end by destroying every pure soul that came near you?

When I first met you I was an innocent boy. By the time we parted, alas! I was the disciple of a devil.

You used to say to me, 'Life is not a rose-strewn path. It is a battle and we must fight.'

But it was not the battle that excited you. It was destruction. The lust for destruction. You loved to destroy things. You weren't happy until you had brought pain and suffering to the boys who loved you, until you had brought them low. But you yourself never fell. That is what made you so frightening, so dangerous.

You love to give alcohol to boys who don't know the taste of liquor and then sit back and watch them suffer. But you don't stop there. You want to watch them as they fall further and further into alcoholism while you yourself never touch a drop.

If you were just a hard-drinking, whore-buying ruffian you may not have posed such a danger. Why? Because you would have been the object of universal contempt. But everyone thought of you as a perfect gentleman (despite the fact that in your case a certain distance from the fair sex was hardly indicative of virtue). This is what made you so dangerous. Those naive and good-hearted boys all trusted you. They became your disciples. And what became of them? Tsuchida-san, I know young men besides myself who were loved by you. And I know how they ended up.

I gained knowledge, but sold my soul. I will have to live with the fact that I sacrificed my body to your strange love, but having sold my soul fills me with regret.

Tsuchida-san, I've allowed myself to voice this bitterness for too long already. There really is no end to this kind of complaint. As I mentioned before, I have not begun this letter in order to criticise you. So let me get to the point.

III

I am not blaming you, but I want to make one thing clear, and that is how much my personality changed because of you.

When I first met you in the grounds of our school I was a vulnerable young boy who wouldn't hurt a fly. But you remember all the horrifying stories you told me every time we met. Before then I'm sure I was completely uninterested in horror, in the bizarre or the criminal. But you found it fascinating to the extreme and introduced me to literature and scholarly works on all of these subjects. Thinking back to it now I see that what you really liked was forcing your own tastes on me and making me drink that poisoned brew. But I knew nothing of this. I trusted you and believed everything you said.

At the time not that many books on horror and crime had been translated into Japanese, so we had no choice but to read them in the original. Somewhere you got your hands on books by authors I had never heard of, such as Poe, Doyle, Freeman and Krafft-Ebing. You gave them to me under the pretence of language study, didn't you? You lectured me on Carpenter, talked of Whitman and introduced me to Montaigne. Run through by every conceivable weapon and forced by you to build up a demonic philosophy, I found myself stimulated by the criminal and the bizarre. And all the while I was your plaything. Tsuchida-san, I was one of your victims. And because I lacked your brilliance, your zeal, your circumspection and, in some cases, your astounding self-possession, I walked straight into the trap life had set me.

You should be happy with yourself. Not only did you mercilessly transform me into your plaything, but now I languish here in prison, while you, who taught me everything, have used your talents and intelligence to go through life without a single misstep. I respect and admire you from the bottom of my heart.

But at the same time I cannot help being appalled at the frailty of the laws of this nation that are powerless to do anything to stop someone as dangerous as you. You are the prosecutor and I am the criminal. What perfect roles for us! But neither you nor I will ever free ourselves from crime, not as long as we live.

By now I'm sure that all of these tedious accusations have given you a sense of why I wanted to tell my story to you in particular. If I hadn't met you that time when I was a boy I would never have ended up in this place. You didn't teach me crime. But you did give me the personality of a criminal. This is what I wanted to tell you above all else.

And there's something else I want you to remember. Surely you do remember it; that autumn evening when we talked of our passionate friendship? If my memory serves, the school year started in September at that time. I had just enrolled, my head was still spinning from the stress of studying for entrance exams, and I was suffering from what seemed a slight bout of neurasthenia.

Life in the dorms was especially unfamiliar to me and each night I found myself almost entirely unable to sleep. This made attending my daily classes an excruciating affair.

It was the 10th October. And once again I had trouble sleeping and went down into the school grounds. Among the dark autumn grasses I caught a fleeting glance of a shadow. That shadow was you.

Until then you and I had never spoken a word to each other. But there is nothing strange in two dormitory mates having a conversation when they find themselves at two in the morning standing in a playground overgrown with autumn grasses. The first thing I said to you was that my nights had been made miserable for the previous month by lack of sleep. You were deeply moved and told me that you yourself had suffered from insomnia for two years already. Under the dark skies our conversation drifted towards those sleepless nights and as we spoke a warm intimacy grew between us. By dawn we were bound together in a beautiful friendship.

But unfortunately I came to resemble you even in your painful sickness. I complained of my suffering each time we met. It was then that I first learned the names of Bromal, Adalin, and Veronal and began to use them regularly. Of course this was also under your guidance. Not surprisingly, this education gave birth to something truly accursed (as I will explain presently). But unlike with your other teachings, you were as much a victim of this one as I was. Recently I heard from a friend that you are now unable to sleep without ingesting enormous quantities of powerful sleeping medication. It is that pain. That pain that I want you in particular to understand.

Tsuchida-san, you, of course, know why I am going on about drugs in this way. To the best of my knowledge I am now in jail for having employed a large dose of powerful medication (of sleeping powder, to be exact) to kill my lover Ishihara Sueko.

I have now committed to paper just those circumstances of which I wanted you to be aware in advance. From this point forward I will write of the crime I did commit and the one I did not. You should know that I do not tell lies. I implore you once more in the name of that friendship we once shared. Please, please believe me.

IV

To order my story properly I should start with the time you and I split up. As I noted earlier, that hot friendship of ours broke off suddenly with your enrolment at university. I would have been twenty at the time. And you were twenty-two.

When you left me for a pretty younger boy I found myself for a time completely bereft. At the same time, as I said earlier, I discovered that you had already breathed your soul into me.

It was in the autumn of that year as well when I met a beautiful woman called Ishihara Sueko.

Tsuchida-san, I had become your disciple in every way, but your particular brand of sensuality seems not to have penetrated me completely. I felt an intense physical desire for Sueko.

It's tedious to have to listen to other people's love stories. Tales of broken hearts must be particularly odious to you since you have not the slightest interest in the opposite sex and abhor sentimentalism. So I'll try to stick to the story line as closely as possible.

Sueko was eighteen at the time, two years younger than I was. She was a student at the XX School for Girls. The first time I saw her it was at the auditorium of a music conservatory in Ueno. You remember don't you? Those concerts that were held every Saturday in Ueno. They were about the only legitimate musical events Tokyo had to offer. There was one other concert series that was sponsored by the family of a famous former daimyo. But you always hated aristocrats so you never took me. Not even once.

Sueko and I were both regulars at those Saturday concerts. The audience were all working people. I won't bore you with the details of how we got together. Let's just say that from that autumn the little forest in Ueno where you and I used to pledge our love to each other became the spot for Sueko and I to do the same. I had just learned how to love the opposite sex. I loved her so much I would have given her everything I had. She seemed quite well disposed towards me as well. If this love affair had a happy ending I might have been able to suck out that awful snake venom you pumped into my veins. I know what you'll never know; how beautiful women are, how precious. Sueko would have been the goddess who saved me.

But the chips didn't fall that way. Our romance came to a nasty end. And the end came much faster than I thought. By the end of that same year a future husband had been found for Sueko.

Whether it was her intention or not – she claimed at the time that she was sacrificing herself to her parents' wishes – made no difference to me. All that mattered was that she had chosen a man other than me to be her husband. I was furious. I was sad. And I cursed women. Tsuchida-san, that's when everything you used to say started to work on me again. I cursed all women.

What I'm about to say isn't easy to talk about. I, the young prodigy, started carousing so much that my friends at university came down on me hard. They told me I was making them all look bad. But what did I care? What value could a warning from my friends have if they didn't understand my suffering? In the spring of my twenty-first year I had to drop out of university.

Thanks to you, up to then everyone thought of me as a brilliant and well-behaved young man. Now my transformation was so extreme that a trusted teacher urged me just to take a break for a while and then come back to university. But I had already made my decision. I threw away that school cap with the two white stripes that was once so precious to me and marched right out of the university gates. It was that time of the year when every tree around the dormitory sent its blossoms scattering like crazy in the spring breeze and everyone was outside enjoying it.

My parents back home were shocked by my rash behaviour. They came to me in tears and begged me to reconsider. But there was no turning back and I had no desire whatsoever to go back to university. Then they got angry and tried to call me back home. But how could someone schooled in your demonic teachings ever set foot in the rustic backwater I came from? I told them they could go to hell and drifted my way through big old Tokyo without any goal in sight.

Over the next few years I tried out all sorts of jobs. Once I got a job at a magazine helping with translations. Once I worked writing film scenarios for the moving pictures. Before long I'd prowled around every last corner of Tokyo.

I had just enough work to eat, but there were two things I could never give up. One was alcohol and the other was sleeping powder. The more I drank the more powder I took. The loss of Sueko made me so self-destructive that I couldn't get to sleep on my own. I was already so far gone that even a double dose wasn't enough.

Eight years have passed since then. You know very well from your own experience how much more of it you have to take after using it for so long. The amount I take now would probably be just right for you since you use it all the time, but it would be enough to kill anyone else.

So to get back to the beginning, I lost Sueko and I dropped out of university. As I started to hear how my classmates were coming up in the world I just sunk deeper into the gutter. About two years ago I started living with a woman. My current wife – who finally got permission to visit me here yesterday. My wife Tsuyuko. Later you'll understand what made that meeting so fateful.

Of course she's not an educated woman. She was working in a real dive of a cafe. Like Sueko, she is two years younger than me and we got to be close when I used to go out drinking.

Tsuyuko loved me. I wasn't that into her. She was fiercely loyal. And kind. So two years ago I married her and we started living together. It wasn't a marriage for love (at least on my side). I needed her devotion, her kindness, her body and the little cash she'd saved up. Tsuchida-san, I say this without any shame: I was a little devil. I'm sure you would agree there was no reason not to sacrifice a dame or two so that I could grow up into a bigger devil.

Tsuyuko didn't have any family so I was all she had. Even after we got married she was obedient, faithful and sweet as could be. I could go out drinking and buy as many whores as I wanted and she couldn't say a word. With such a loveable wife I finally felt at peace.

V

Six relatively peaceful months passed with my new wife, interrupted only by the death of my father. Of course I hurried home as soon as I got the news but he died before I arrived. I was the heir so a little property came my way. Not much but enough for the two of us to get by, so I returned to Tokyo.

I started working at the magazine again doing translations and set myself up with a little income. I was renting a small house in the suburbs at the time and have lived there ever since. Anyone would have thought this young couple had the world on a string. I even thought so myself.

But alas, that was just a daydream. I'd forgotten that I was the disciple of a devil. After that first six months Tsuyuko started to get on my nerves. Of course I didn't marry her for love and I was never crazy about her, but I had never hated her either.

Once we started living together, however, I began to despise her. Of course all young couples start to get on each other's nerves once the honeymoon period is over. But in my case it was different. I told you already that Tsuyuko was obedient, faithful and sweet. Now it was those same qualities – that same obedience, faithfulness and sweetness – that started to grate on me. I hated her for her shyness. Her girlish virtue irritated me. And more than anything that sweet disposition drove me out of my mind.

It was then that I felt the seed you planted inside me start to grow. I was afraid of myself. I felt like I had to do something. But I didn't know how to escape this strange agony.

Tsuchida-san, you have no interest in the opposite sex so you are no doubt still single. You probably cannot imagine the suffering of a husband who hates his wife. But as my mentor you do of course understand what it's like to hate someone who is blameless in the eyes of the world, someone who has nothing but good qualities.

I tried to get rid of Tsuyuko but she wouldn't leave me. She didn't mind if there was another woman. Said she'd work as a maid as long as she could stay by my side. Since there was no talking her into leaving I tried all kinds of ways to make her want to leave on her own. But nothing worked. Physical and psychological abuse had no effect. In fact the more I tried to push her away the more she clung to me and wormed her way further in. I couldn't stand to be near her.

If she'd been a little less of a good girl, a bit more selfish, if she'd just pushed back a little I might not have been so enraged. But she never let up. She was demure and obedient no matter what. I could stay out three or four nights in a row and she wouldn't say a word when I came home. Not a word until bedtime that is, when she would get down on her knees and beg me to love her. The pathetic sight of her was nauseating. I hated her so much I wanted to tear her into shreds and eat her. I would make a point of sending her out on errands on stormy nights but she just kept on smiling. When I couldn't stand it any more I would slap the smile off her face. But Tsuyuko just bawled and begged me to love her more.

I did everything I could think of to turn her body and soul into an instrument for my own pleasure, my toy. I thought surely this would get her to cave in. But she held fast. In the end I tortured her so cruelly that I started to hate myself. I started to feel possessed by her living ghost.

Tsuchida-san, if you'd been in this situation I'm sure you would have used that powerful brain of yours and found a solution. But heaven didn't bless me with a brain like yours and what I came up with was pretty damn prosaic. There was only one way for me. It was death. To die. And according to our philosophy she was the one who had to go. Sometimes late at night she used to say she'd kill herself if I left her. I'd tell her, 'Go ahead. Knock yourself off for all I care.' But I was only saying it to hurt her. I never thought it might actually happen.

But as the days wore on the idea started to grow on me. I imagined what it would be like to have Tsuyuko dead. I still had trouble sleeping but I comforted myself by picturing her dying by illness, by suicide or by murder. I don't know how many nights I indulged in these devilish fantasies with the hateful sound of Tsuyuko's breathing next to me. Tsuyuko's face as she slept filled me with satisfaction and I smiled as I gazed upon it.

What do you think, Tsuchida-san? Had I not become the perfect inheritor of your soul?

VI

At that time I was still just fantasising about murdering my wife. I had no intention of actually carrying it out. But then something happened that made everything change. Ishihara Sueko and I met again.

I imagine a woman-hater like you will laugh at the thought of someone who hates his first love but still can't stop thinking of her. But it can't be helped. This is the difference between your personality and mine. I lost her when I was twenty but I always, always remembered her.

As I drifted around the country I was careful to follow what news I could find about the famous, rich man she had married. So I knew that he had been killed during the Great Kanto Earthquake, crushed mercilessly beneath a building along with virtually every other member of her family and the neighbourhood they lived in.

But my masculine pride kept me from going to see her. And even if I wanted to see her I couldn't have since I didn't know where she lived. And then, towards the end of last summer, I bumped into her in a section of Yamanote. She told me that she had been living there alone with only a maid to keep her company since the earthquake had taken her husband. Bereft of everything, from the family she had married into, to the town they lived in, she had lost all hope.

We talked about the way things used to be. We went back to the days we had spent together. I truly loved her and she loved me. Sometime between the autumn and winter of last year our passionate love came back in full force.

Of course I told my wife Tsuyuko all about it. I figured this would be more than enough to get her to leave me. Wrong again. She didn't budge from what she'd said before. I could fall as much in love with other women as I wanted, just as long as I didn't leave her.

I figured things could be worse and stayed away from home for most of the final months of last year, shacked up with Sueko the whole time. Luckily Sueko didn't have any children. She didn't know for sure if I was married or not. And anyway I promised to marry her eventually. You're probably wondering why I didn't just dump Tsuyuko. Perfectly understandable. Tsuyuko was alive but she haunted me like a ghost. As long as she was alive there was no escaping her. No matter how long I stayed away from home she'd be waiting there when I came back with that same pathetic and yet accursed look on her face.

By February of this year I had resolved to kill her. In January she had started to feel sick and February brought no improvement. Turns out she was pregnant. She was carrying my seed.

What awful luck. Your typical husband – no, anyone human – would be thrilled to have made his wife pregnant. But not me. I found it revolting and terrifying. The wife I hated and despised was pregnant with my seed. I knew myself too well not to realise it was the devil's seed that was growing inside her. It was bad enough that the bitch was pregnant. But this was the spawn of a devil. I had to kill her and I had to do it fast. I had to get out of this nightmare.

I wanted to kill her partly to rid myself of her living ghost. I knew she would keep haunting me wherever I ran. But now that she was pregnant it was even worse. I was done for as long as she was alive. I could try to hide from her but she'd hold on until the kid was born. But the thought of her giving birth to this cursed child sent shivers down my spine. This second me born from Tsuyuko would pursue me for the rest of my life. I had to stop her from having this child. I had to bury her and the child inside her.

I have to admit I found the thought of killing her thrilling. I'd made up my mind. She had to be killed. And now all was left was to figure out how and when.

VII

Once I'd made up my mind I used every moment not spent enjoying myself with Sueko thinking up methods of murder. I hunted down every book I could find for ideas on how to kill people. I went back and reread all the books you recommended when we were in secondary school. I researched all the cleverest ways of committing murder.

The first thing I learned was that you can't even get started until you have got rid of your conscience. The annals of crime teach us that it's the conscience that catches murderers. They might be brave and bold when they do the deed, but they become cowards afterwards. Case after case shows us that the murderer would never have been caught if he had kept his cool after the act.

At least on this point I was very optimistic. I was the devil's disciple. I ought to have lost whatever I had of a conscience. But since I couldn't be sure until I'd actually committed the murder, I decided there was no use worrying about it now. I commanded myself to be bold and to stay strong once the deed was done.

Then there was the question of the method. This was crucial.

Certain murderers and criminals you read about in detective novels put a great deal of effort into disposing of the body. This is a waste of effort as far I'm concerned. If you can't lay your hands on the chemicals Dorian Gray used to destroy that painter's corpse there's no point racking your brains over the method of disposal. Just leave the body lying there like it is. As long as nobody knows it's a murder it won't make a bit of difference. Of course you don't want to try too hard to make it look like a suicide. This is an instance where gilding the lily can be fatal. It's enough just to keep people from suspecting foul play.

Next I had to choose the best method to knock her off. My research told me that the best place to do it was at home. It would be too dangerous to take her off somewhere else to kill her. The best is to do it right there in the comfortable surroundings of home.

Finally, the ideal method would be one where the victim doesn't notice even if you fail the first time around. If you screw up the first time you can just put on a poker face and wait for your next chance. And if that doesn't work you aim for another opportunity. You can try as many times as it takes and eventually you'll succeed.

But was there such a method? You're a veritable genius in this sort of thing so I'm sure, had you been in my place, you would have seen that the perfect method was staring me in the face and would have wasted no time putting it into action.

But I didn't see it.

Before long, February was over and it was the middle of March.

During this time I went back to Tsuyuko's once every ten days or so but otherwise I was living with Sueko. Before long I had stocked Sueko's house with all the things I needed on a daily basis.

But then the moment came. The way to kill Tsuyuko came to me like a dark suggestion, and it came right out of Tsuyuko's own mouth.

VIII

It was the 25th March. For the first time in ages I had left Sueko's and come back to my wife's place. I don't know what was going on in her head but like always she didn't complain. We sat facing each other after this long absence and once I'd finished eating the shitty meal she'd prepared I dived back into my research on murder.

At the time I never got to sleep before midnight so I told Tsuyuko to go to sleep without me. Always the obedient wife, she slipped into the futon without a word. I thought she'd gone to sleep there beside me but before long she started to cry. Not again, I thought, and felt myself getting irritated as usual. I kept silent but then she started whining.

'Eizō, honey, I've been having trouble sleeping lately. I didn't get a wink of sleep last night and I'm still not even tired.'

'Is that so?' I said, just to get her to shut up. I could not have cared less whether she could sleep or not.

But then I replayed her words in my mind. *I've been having trouble sleeping lately.* It was like a bolt of lightning. 'That's it!' I screamed into the night. And I didn't care who heard. Of course! This was it. All my thinking, all my planning had been leading up to this all along. She'd given me the answer herself.

Tomorrow your life is over bitch. Tomorrow your suffering will come to an end. Tomorrow night I'll put you out of your misery!

Before I go on I should fill you in on how much sleeping medication I needed to get to sleep and how I got my hands on it. As I'm sure you can imagine from your own experience, the regular sleeping medication they have at the pharmacy doesn't have the slightest effect on me any more. So much so that the idea of committing suicide with Calmochine just makes me laugh.

After trying one medicine after another without any success I ended up in the office of a famous doctor who prescribed me a certain sleeping medication in powder form. But he told me that in cases like these (of insomnia) it's better that the patient not know what's in the medicine he's taking. Apparently it doesn't work nearly as well if you know the ingredients. So he said he wouldn't tell me under any circumstances and had it prepared specially by a pharmacist in the neighbourhood. All I could gather was that it was a kind of cocktail, a mixture of several different kinds of medicine. At first I dutifully picked up three days' worth of the medicine at a time and took it as the doctor prescribed.

You've been an insomniac longer than I have, so you know that this kind of relationship with the pharmacist doesn't last long. Six months passed and a single day's dose was no longer enough. I thought about it and figured I'd try a double dose. It worked like a charm. But then I had to go back to the pharmacist for more. I needed an excuse so I used the one that all of us insomniacs stumble upon eventually. You know what I'm talking about.

'I spilled the package.'

This fooled him the first time but I could hardly do it again.

'I'm going on a trip for a week.'

That got me another batch, so I was able to take two or two and a half times the daily dosage. I couldn't get to sleep without it. But pharmacists are businessmen after all. I'd been going to this one for quite a while so he trusted me all right. I would go through a ten-day supply in three days and he kept quiet about it. Before long I was taking scary amounts of the stuff just to get through the night. Once they get to this point insomniacs have to have extra medicine on hand or they get really anxious. The more money I handed over to the pharmacist each month, the more medicine I needed just to keep my head on straight.

Last autumn, when I started staying with Sueko most of the time I decided I needed to keep a supply at her house too. I had the pharmacist in my back pocket by this time and I got him to give me two small bottles full of that powerful white powder. I kept one of them at home and the other at Sueko's place, helping myself to two or three teaspoons whenever I needed it.

Tsuchida-san, I hear you're increasing your dosage as well. But I guess not even a genius like you can see where you'll end up.

Now I'm using ten times the amount that the doctor prescribed for me two years ago. Even then the dose was many times stronger than what any normal person would need. But now it's ten times that. What kind of effect would that have on a delicate pregnant woman? I thought about it for a while and decided that even if I couldn't kill her with such a big dose at once it would be enough to do irreversible damage. And it would be so easy to get her to take it. She knew nothing about drugs so all I had to do was make sure she was watching when I took my regular dose. She would take the same amount thinking it was safe. And that would be that.

If she vomited or something else went wrong I would make sure that she saw me taking the same amount again so she wouldn't have any reason for suspicion. So there was no danger even if my plan failed. And if everything went right it would look like she had overdosed by mistake. Even considering the fact that Sueko was my mistress and I had a motive for killing

Tsuyuko, who could prove that I had forced her to take the medicine? The only problem left was my own conscience. As long as I denied everything I was sure I'd go scot-free.

My plan was made. Now all I had to do was carry it out.

IX

The thought that I was going to kill my wife the next day was so arousing that I hardly slept on the night of the 25th. But the day dawned and it was the 26th. I hurried over to Sueko's house. Since I wouldn't be staying with her that night I wanted to spend at least a little time with her.

After a few precious hours with Sueko I got ready to go back home in the early afternoon. And then she said it.

'Are you leaving already? I wish you'd stay over tonight. I've been having trouble sleeping lately.'

I shuddered at the thought of this bizarre coincidence. But I told her I had some business to attend to and left. Now I look back and realise this was to be our final parting.

I arrived back home that afternoon and Tsuyuko, who had assumed I'd be gone for much longer, was overjoyed to see me. I made a special effort to be nice to her, knowing that this was the last day we would spend together.

Before long that awful night had arrived: the night of the 26th. My preparations were meticulous. Not being a doctor I can't say I know for sure, but in my own experience sleeping medication works best on an empty stomach.

At dinner I said to Tsuyuko, 'You shouldn't eat too much or you won't be able to sleep.' She was so pleased by this unexpected bit of kindness on my part that she ate only a single bowl of rice. As darkness finally fell it was time to act.

At the time I was still trying to figure out exactly how much medicine it would take to do the job. But since I knew nothing about medicine (not to mention the fact that I had no idea what kind of medicine I was taking) I had to make a guess. To be sure, I decided to get her to take the same amount as I did: five teaspoons of powder, enough to last ten days. It was around ten-thirty.

'If you can't sleep why don't you have some of my medicine? I'm going to have some now. You have some too.' I said this as nonchalantly as possible.

'Yes,' she said, submissive as always, and spread the futon on the floor.

That's right! So far so good.

Once she finished putting out the futon and came to sit opposite me at the brazier I took out the packet of medicine and made sure she was watching as I downed five teaspoons one after another. Agitated as I was I started to think even this would not be enough to put me to sleep so I took one more spoonful and gave Tsuyuko a piece of paper on which I had measured out five spoonfuls. She stared at the medicine without saying anything and suddenly an idea occurred to me.

Looking back on it now I realise that I was just courting disaster with this bright idea. But at the time I thought it was brilliant.

My idea was to let someone know that Tsuyuko was still awake when I went to sleep. This could be very important just in case anyone should suspect me of having drugged her.

'Run down to the Konoe-ya and get me three packs of Airships.'

There was a tobacconist a couple of blocks away from our house called Konoe-ya. The owner was there all the time. He was a chess partner of mine and we often had a game together in our off time. Because of this I usually went there to buy cigarettes myself. So if Tsuyuko went now he was sure to ask how I was.

'What's your husband up to?' he was sure to say, just out of politeness. And Tsuyuko would answer, 'He's just gone to sleep actually.'

If anyone should investigate later the owner of the Konoe-ya could testify that I had gone to sleep before my wife. This would make it look like she had overdosed accidentally. I congratulated myself for thinking up such a brilliant plan.

Tsuyuko obeyed this order as meekly as ever. She folded the paper with the medicine, and tucked it into her *obi*. I kept staring at the medicine, at that little paper package that was poking its head half-way out of her *obi*. *Soon that will be in her stomach and everything will be over. What fragile creatures people are!*

Before long Tsuyuko got up and went out through the kitchen to buy the cigarettes.

While she was gone I moved into the bedroom and got into my futon. My wife's futon is next to mine, waiting for its occupant to return. Tomorrow it will hold a corpse.

I lay in my own futon and waited for Tsuyuko to return. But then I started to feel the powerful effects of the medicine. I felt very sleepy. I had taken more of it than ever before. To make matters worse I'd taken it on an empty stomach since I had no appetite earlier in the evening. I was vaguely aware of the sound of Tsuyuko banging the kitchen door closed when she got back. But then, it seems, I fell into a deep sleep.

I don't know how long I slept, but suddenly I was awake and staring at the ceiling, feeling somehow heavy all over. I feel like the back of my head is wrapped up in something. And I've got a headache. This always happens after I've taken a little too much sleeping medication.

I glance at my watch and it's four-thirty. I raise my head and see that the shutters are flung wide open.

I lie there in a daze for a while, but then the light through the *shōji* makes me realise it is evening.

And then, suddenly, the memory of the night before came rushing back to me.

I gave her the medicine! She must have taken it!
That's right. I tried to kill Tsuyuko!

My wife? Tsuyuko?

I looked around. She ought to have been lying there next to me in this room. But she's not there. Even the futon has been put away.

I leapt to my feet. I threw open the sliding door to the living room. There she was, looking like she had just come out of the kitchen, ever the dutiful wife. She looked a little sad as usual, but otherwise she was as calm as could be.

'You're awake! You were sleeping so soundly I tried to keep quiet. But it's already five o'clock you know.'

I started to say something. But my mouth was dry and nothing came out.

'You… you got to sleep last night?'

'No, I didn't sleep very well.'

'But you took the medicine didn't you?'

'Yes. I took it.'

'You took all of it? You took what I gave you?'

'No, silly. If I took that much it would kill me.'

A sweet smile played on Tsuyuko's lips as she said this. From the look on her face she seemed almost to pity me in my ignorance.

'I don't know if you realise it or not, but you're taking way too much of that stuff. When you stay away for so long I have trouble sleeping myself so I've been going to the pharmacy to get some of my own medicine. I knew you would be furious if I so much as touched yours. And the pharmacist told me lots of things. He was shocked when I told him how much of it you take and he said I should try to get you to cut back a little. But you get so angry when I say the wrong thing. So I just kept my worries to myself. I divided the medicine you gave me yesterday into ten parts and just took one of them. If I'd taken all of it I think it would have killed me. Last night something was upsetting me and I couldn't sleep after all. But you went straight to sleep didn't you? Oh, yes. The Airships you asked for are on your desk.'

It felt like someone had hit me over the head. Sweet little Tsuyuko has no idea that she was almost murdered. She hasn't noticed that her evil husband, the one standing in front of her right now, just tried to kill her.

Tsuchida-san. I don't know anything about the law so I'm not sure whether this would be called an attempted murder – but let's say it is. If this had been the end of it no one would ever have known about this attempted murder and the whole thing would have ended in a farce.

But events were proceeding along a much more frightening path than that.

X

Tsuyuko knew all about the medicine. She knew about it but she never said a word! I had failed to kill her. Luckily my plan was so airtight that she didn't know how close she'd come to being murdered, but it was a big blow nonetheless.

I didn't have an ounce of compassion for her. In fact I hated her all the more. I started to think the bitch knew what I was up to and was just playing dumb. Then I couldn't stand being around her for a second longer.

I turned my back on that surprised look on her face, changed out of my pyjamas, stuffed the Airships she'd fetched the night before into my sleeve and stormed out of the house.

I was on fire inside. I failed to kill my wife! I wasn't even relieved to think the woman hadn't noticed. I was mortified and so furious I could hardly contain myself.

I don't know where I went or how I got there. All I know is that I stumbled from one seedy cafe to another and downed as much strong liquor as I could. Finally I ended up at Sueko's. I wanted to see my beautiful, my darling Sueko. I got to her house by about seven in the evening. I'd had so many stiff drinks that I was weaving all over the place.

When I got there, in front of her house, something weird was going on. It was normally a quiet neighbourhood but now there were cars all around and lots of people milling about.

At first I didn't notice that they were all hanging around Sueko's house, but it became obvious as I got closer.

I stood there in shock. Something's slamming against my chest. Something has happened. I push my way through the crowd that has gathered around the latticework door.

Just as I was getting to the entrance a man in a suit and tie came out of the house talking to another man wearing what looked like a police uniform. I can remember exactly what the man in the suit said to the other.

'What a mess. You folks will have to figure out whether it was an accident or suicide, but she had some powerful medicine in a bottle right next to her. Looks like she took it with that spoon. Crazy stuff. She's done for, of course. Her heart's stopped.'

I knew straightaway that something had happened to Sueko and pushed my way past the startled crowd into the room I knew so well.

Tsuchida-san, of course you know what I found there.

There, beneath sheets that seemed to smoulder my beautiful Sueko lay dead. She was like a white statue laid down to sleep, sprawled on her back with her right hand stretched out on top of the futon.

When I came to my senses the man standing next to me was grabbing me by the collar.

'Who are you?'

'I know this woman.'

As I spoke, I ran my eyes over Sueko's corpse like I was licking it. I saw the fruit of my research into the methods of murder.

Strangely enough, at the time I didn't feel like I was looking at the body of someone I'd lost. It was just a bizarre lump of happy-making flesh. And it was the result of all my planning.

And then I lost it. A wave of nausea swept over me as I yelled out, 'You're wrong! She was murdered. Somebody drugged her. Who would ever take it by mistake?'

I repeated these words over and over as I ran out of Sueko's house, away from the gawking crowd.

XI

Sueko was dead. I had lost the one I loved, forever!

I went home that night like a man without a soul. But how could I stay with my wife? How could I hold on in this world full of pain? I decided to escape from this hateful existence as soon as I possibly could.

That night I threw myself onto a train at Iidamachi Station. I was headed for that desolate village in Kiso where you and I went for summer vacation. I wanted to say goodbye to the world from there.

It was the 27th March. As I settled down on the train, alone, I began to feel like myself again. I started to think about why things had ended up this way.

It wasn't hard to guess. It was Sueko who knew nothing about drugs. She must have seen me take the stuff when I stayed at her house. Last night she couldn't sleep alone, so the ignorant woman took that strong medicine just like I did. When evening came and she still hadn't woken up the little maid panicked and ran to the doctor. And then the whole mess began.

I thought of a million things for more than ten hours as the train swayed me back and forth. And I got all sentimental at having lost Sueko forever.

But then I remembered the strange attraction of Sueko's flesh-turned-corpse and in the dark train I imagined the figures and flesh of lots of women.

It was just before noon on the 28th that I arrived in X Station in Kiso. I checked into that small hotel where you and I stayed together. And I thought about my future.

What a bizarre coincidence! The wife I hate and the woman I love! And when will I ever get any sleep now?

I can't stand this pain anymore. The only escape is death or insanity. I made up my mind. This day, 28th March, would see me dead or see me insane.

And the sleeping medication I have is just the thing. I'm going to down the whole bottle. Even if it doesn't kill me I certainly won't wake up in the same shape I am now. That's what I was thinking.

I thought I would leave behind a record of my crimes. So I spent the whole day writing down my plans to kill Tsuyuko.

By ten at night I was finally done.

I was about to take the medicine but then I thought again.

There's no reason to leave a note. It's more interesting to leave behind a crime that will never be solved. I burned everything that I had just written. Or rather, I thought I burned everything.

It was then that I was visited by yet another bizarre coincidence. I was anything but calm at the time and even though I thought I burned the whole letter I didn't notice that part of it remained intact – the part that described what happened between the time I decided to kill Tsuyuko and the time I set out to do it. It was the section that begins, 'I decided I had to get away from her. Somehow I had to kill her,' and ends with, 'She probably doesn't know anything about medicine, so she won't notice if I get her to take it.' 'I took my dose in front of her. She watched in silence. I measured out the same amount and gave it to her.'

If I had written 'my wife' or 'Tsuyuko' instead of 'her', this letter would not be evidence of a murder plot. My failure to write her name brought about an unexpected consequence.

I swallowed the whole bottle of sleeping powder after I finished writing that letter. I said my last goodbyes to this hateful world and the sound of the water in the Kiso River became my funeral dirge.

Tsuchida-san. I would have been so happy if I had died then. But I suppose I had yet to repay my sins.

38

XII

I soon fell into a river of sleep. I have no idea for how many hours or days I slept. When I opened my eyes and looked around, my head throbbing with pain and overcome by a wave of nausea, I found myself in what I now know to have been a police headquarters near the X Station in Kiso.

The cops must have followed me after I shot off my mouth at Sueko's place. The people at the inn in X Village must have alerted the local police when I didn't wake up for so long.

In any case, I woke up from a tortured sleep in an unfamiliar place. I was in sorry shape.

I'm sure you know how unpleasant it is to wake up after taking even a small overdose of sleeping medication. But I had taken twenty days' worth or more in a single dose. It was a miracle that I had come back to life at all. So you won't be surprised to hear that I had lost all memory and all powers of understanding.

I was like a man without a soul and it was in this condition that I found myself loaded onto the train. Now I know that I was being sent back to Tokyo.

Until that point I was unable to give a coherent answer to any of the questions they asked me. Everything was clouded in mist. I could not understand myself. Or, to put it in more extreme terms, I could not even recall clearly who I was.

It seems they had a doctor look after me for a time after I came back here. He must have determined at some point that there was nothing physically wrong with me, so I found myself sitting across from a police detective.

Right off I was confronted with those unburned pages of the suicide note I had written in Kiso.

'Looks familiar doesn't it, mate? You wrote it, right?'

I stared at them for a while without saying anything. It was my handwriting all right. After a while I started to remember having written them. But aside from that I drew a complete blank.

'Don't play stupid, wise guy!'

I don't know how many times I heard those words. But I wasn't playing dumb. At the time, I mean all the way up to yesterday, I had no clear memory of the facts. That powerful drug had robbed me of the ability to think and to remember.

After they showed me my suicide note I sat in my cell alone and tried to think. At a certain point I dredged up the memory of Sueko; dead Sueko, looking so beautiful I wanted to eat her up. Her right hand stretched out, face up in her futon. Dead, but looking for all the world like she was asleep.

Ahh. The girl is dead. I tried to kill her. That's it. I was thinking of how to get her to take the medicine. And then…

Slowly, the gears started turning in my enfeebled brain and settled on the idea that I myself might have killed her.

Then I started to talk about how I felt, pulling together the delicate threads of my memory. But I couldn't come up with much detail. I couldn't remember when I'd met her or why I wanted to kill her.

They must have had evidence placing me at Sueko's house that day. At some point they put me before an examining judge.

But how was I supposed to tell the judge anything more than what I had said already? All I could do was answer his questions with yes or no.

I didn't know myself whether I had killed her or not.

If I hadn't been in confinement the stimulation of the outside world might have jogged my memory earlier. But I spent every day inside my jail cell. Even had I tried to remember, I couldn't.

Then, one day, a strange thing happened.

My wife Tsuyuko finally got permission and came to visit me.

You might find this hard to believe, but up until that point I had forgotten that I even had a wife.

The sight of her sad, timid face across from me gave me an uncanny feeling. But then my eyes were riveted to the *obi* of her kimono.

There's a piece of paper tucked into her obi. Now I realise that she'd probably just been to the doctor for it. *It's a paper packet of sleeping powder, peeking half-way out of her obi.*

Then it hit me like a bolt of lightning.

That's it! That's it! The obi! *The paper!*

I've seen it somewhere before. I must have seen it somewhere before!

When? Where?

Still as a stone I sat staring at the paper packet.

Like a man possessed I wrung every drop of memory from my brain.

That's it! I tried to kill this woman. She's the one, Tsuyuko. She was my intended victim.

Storms, thunder, and lightning raged on inside my brain. And without a word to Tsuyuko, I fled back to my cell.

I mustn't forget this. Don't forget what you just remembered!

I spent all day yesterday and all night last night trying to remember the whole story.

Tsuchida-san, the awful truths I have written here are what I managed to reconstruct after a night spent remembering and tracing the trail of my thoughts.

That's right. These are the facts and there is no mistaking them. I wanted to kill my wife. I didn't try to kill Sueko. Nor did I kill her.

From what I can tell, Sueko died by accident.

Once I recovered my memory fully, I recalled that you, my old friend, happened to be in the prosecutor's office of this very court.

You may be the only person who will believe what I have recounted here. I know I can count on you to believe that nothing I have said here is untrue.

The facts may be incredible but facts are facts. There's no changing that.

As I mentioned before, I am about to meet with the examining judge and explain the whole situation to him. Most likely, this will clear me of the suspicion of having murdered Ishihara Sueko. Indeed, it must clear me.

But I cannot escape my responsibility towards Tsuyuko in the eyes of the law. Nor do I intend to escape.

Please forgive me for taxing your patience with such a long-winded letter. Tsuchida-san. Three times I call out to you in the name of that friendship we once shared. Please believe me. And in believing me, please believe what I say.

Did He Kill Them?

I

If I were a detective novelist like you gentlemen, I would take this story I'm about to tell you and fashion it into a gripping novel. But seeing as I am just a humble barrister, I'm afraid I'd end up botching the job and making a fool out of myself. So I'm just going to tell the whole thing to you exactly the way it happened. And when I've finished my tale I want to read you a strange manuscript that has never yet seen the light of day. Of course my involvement in this case was as a barrister so my account of it will not include any suppositions or speculations aside from the facts I was able to gather in that capacity. For this reason it may not be as interesting as the novels you write, but if you do find it interesting I encourage any one of you to write it up and publish it. I think it's a story worth telling.

I'll start with the basic timeline of the case. The case in question is that tragic event that occurred one night at the height of summer last year in the town of 'K' in Sagami. The Tokyo newspapers were all over it at the time so I'm sure you have all heard of it, but allow me to review it again from the beginning to help jog your memory.

Last year, on the night of 16th August, or to be more precise around one-thirty on the morning of the 17th – some of you may remember there was a terrible storm that night in the Tokyo area – a terrible tragedy took place at a villa in the busy resort town of 'K'. Now 'K' has always been well known as a spot for bathing and a place to escape the heat but lately it has become even more lively as people from the upper and middle classes have begun to build houses there. In summertime, in particular, it's full of all the smartest people from Tokyo. So it was all the more shocking that something so horrific should happen at such a jolly place.

The incident took place at the villa of a young businessman by the name of Oda Seizō. The victims were Oda himself (who was thirty-three years old at the time) and his wife Michiko (who was twenty-four). Sometime over the course of that night both of them lost their lives in a gruesome fashion.

Oda's father had amassed a tidy fortune in the trading business, but he died when Seizō was still in secondary school and the mother was left to raise the boy on her own. Seizō was always a little sickly and ended up dropping out of college in order to take care of his health. Of course he was kept fairly busy managing all that money, but he had his mother handle most things and spent most of his time at the villa in 'K'. He was spoiled and self-centered like most people brought up with lots of money and it didn't help that he had also been coddled all of his life because of his delicate constitution. But he was also a quiet type and was not known to have quarrelled with people. He had no close friends and seems to have led a rather lonely life despite all his money. At the end of the year before he died, his lungs started to get worse and he suffered a bout of neurasthenia as well, so he and his wife holed up in the place in 'K' and never came to Tokyo.

Michiko was the daughter of a well-known university professor named Kawakami who passed away some years ago. She was wise even as a child and a real beauty to boot. Some of you may even have had the pleasure of meeting her. From the moment she took up residence in 'K' she was said to be the queen of the place. For a barrister like me it's hard to find words to describe her, but let's just say she was extremely beautiful and liberally endowed with what these days goes by the name of 'sexual appeal'. She was known for her beauty since her days as a student at a girls' school and it was said that one look at her would make a devotee out of anyone. As a result she attracted a crowd of young admirers. Since the death of her father had left

46

her quite to her own devices, these young admirers, particularly the male ones, had only increased in number. Among them was a young count, a bachelor with a taste for music, with whom she was often to be seen strolling through the Ginza. There was also an important politician's son with literary ambitions in whose company she often went to the theatre. This aroused the envy of many and gave rise to widespread speculation as to who would be lucky enough to marry her. As the lovely daughter of a distinguished professor whose sensibilities were refined by music and literature, who ran in such rarefied circles and whose elegant comportment was beyond reproach, it was generally assumed that she had but to choose whether she would become a countess, marry into a powerful political family or perhaps become the fashionable wife of a captain of industry.

Thus it was no small surprise to many people when three years ago she suddenly married Oda Seizō. Of course there was no reason to think it was not a proper match given that the gentleman was extremely wealthy and the lady a great beauty and the daughter of an influential family. But these were not the points that made the match so puzzling.

The puzzling fact was that the two barely knew each other before they were married. In other words, theirs was an arranged marriage in the traditional Japanese style. For those who knew Michiko well this was understandably unfathomable. Why on earth would a modern woman like her agree to such a marriage? The news of her engagement came as a great disappointment to all those who prided themselves on knowing Michiko.

But despite all the astonishment it occasioned, the negotiations between the two families proceeded apace and soon the couple was joined in matrimony.

Among those who knew Michiko there were some who assumed that the marriage was not of her own choosing – that despite the prosperous appearance of her family they must have fallen on hard times and Michiko had been sacrificed and married off to the man for his money. And indeed this was not a baseless speculation. Wise women in particular are apt to think this way.

II

The first year of their marriage left little grist for gossip. The young couple seemed to be leading a perfectly placid and peaceful domestic life. And yet the fact that Mrs Oda had continued to socialise with her young male friends did raise a few eyebrows.

After a year Seizō suffered from a serious bout of pleurisy and was confined to his bed for six months. After this the couple stopped going out in the town of 'K' and led a quiet domestic life enlivened only by the company of their servants.

It was just at that time that strange rumours began to circulate to the effect that Michiko was leading a pitiable existence. For one thing it was rumoured that her husband Seizō not only did not love her, but failed to understand her as well. And for another it appeared that, having the kind of temper that often comes with chronic illness, he often abused her verbally and sometimes even struck her. On a number of occasions the servants were said to have witnessed the master of the house in the act of beating his wife.

Michiko was said to suffer her husband's violent behaviour and to be getting along as well as she could. Many began to pity Michiko as a result of these rumours – all the more so because it made her habitual cheerfulness seem like an attempt to put a brave face on her situation. Of course she did confess to a few close friends how perfectly horrid her married life had become and when this information did eventually become more widely known it came as no surprise to most people. Everyone simply reconfirmed their belief that nothing good could come from an arranged marriage, and much less so one motivated by money. As people's sympathy for Michiko increased, her husband and her mother, who had sacrificed her for financial gain, suffered a corresponding decline in the public's estimation.

But before another six months had passed Michiko herself became the subject of unsavoury rumours.

For despite the fact that Seizō was said to be abusing his wife, it was also clear from Michiko's manner that he was in no way restricting her movements. Perhaps it was the fact that her husband was completely ignoring her that enabled her to have such an attitude. But however indifferent her husband might be to her free ways, they were of a nature that the rest of society could hardly fail to notice.

Michiko thought of her home as a cold prison and there were many who felt pity for her and wondered how she could stand it. But on the other hand her behaviour had a negative effect on her reputation. People began to criticise her for associating with young students. And there were even some who said quite openly that there was one among them to whom she was especially close. But Michiko acted as if she were completely unaware of what was being said about her. Her husband Seizō, for his part, was even less concerned than Michiko, or at least he appeared so.

The exact nature of Michiko's misbehaviour was to be exposed unexpectedly as a result of the tragedy.

In this way the young ill-matched couple made their home in 'K' amidst a cloud of rumour and innuendo. Such was their life until the incident occurred.

It was on 16th August of last year, in the afternoon, that two men came to call at the Oda home in 'K'. They had both known the Odas for two or three years at that point. One was a twenty-five year old student of 'K' University called Tomoda Takeshi. The other was Ōtera Ichirō, a student of another university who was twenty-four at the time. Tomoda had attended the same school as Oda Seizō and was himself the scion of an important family. He happened to be renting a villa on the outskirts of 'K' at the time. But he felt lonely there by himself and had come to the Odas' that afternoon in search of company. Ōtera was a student at the university where Michiko's late father had taught. But this Ōtera lived in circumstances very different from Tomoda. It would only come to light later, but it seems that Ōtera's father had benefited from the generosity of Michiko's father. The former was stubborn by nature and had what might be called a mania for suing people. He was always getting himself involved in legal disputes and soon exhausted what small property he had and died while Ichirō was still in secondary school. His mother died soon thereafter leaving relatives to scramble to help him go to university at least. Eventually they appealed to Michiko's family and arranged for him to go to Tokyo to study. At the time of the incident he was three years out of secondary school and, with the help of all kinds of people, was studying at a university in Tokyo and living in a boarding house in the suburbs. He was in the middle of his summer vacation on the day in question and, having been acquainted with the Odas for some time, had come to 'K' for the day to go swimming. I should mention here that both Tomoda and Ōtera happened to be quite close – perhaps too close it was said – to Michiko.

On that afternoon Tomoda and Ōtera had gone swimming in the ocean with Michiko but, as I mentioned earlier, the evening brought a violent storm. The sky began to look quite ominous and the two young men quickly heeded Michiko's warning to get out of the water.

It seems that Seizō was having one of his rare good days. When the two guests returned from the ocean he said, 'Since there are four of us why don't we have a game of mahjong?' Being regulars at the Oda home in 'K', the two guests were enthusiastic mahjong players and needed no persuading.

The game began after dinner – as all of those who were questioned later confirmed – at five-thirty in the evening and ended after about half an hour. Right after dinner the four gathered around the table and started clacking and banging away at the tiles. Meanwhile the weather was worsening outside into a proper storm.

I'm not too familiar with mahjong, but people say it takes some time to get through a game even for accomplished players. Apparently they started out agreeing that they would play two matches (comprising eight 'rounds') back to back. But when those two matches were over the weather wasn't letting up and Michiko was winning. Seizō was dead last and uncharacteristically caught up in the game. He hated to lose and proposed another four rounds, which they played, bringing the total to twelve.

By the time all the rounds were over it was almost midnight. The wind had stopped but the rain was still falling and the husband and wife urged their guests to stay the night. Tomoda had a house in 'K' so begged off and went home by car. Ōtera, on the other hand, decided to take them up on their offer of hospitality since the trains had stopped running and the weather was so bad. According to the maids it was just after midnight when the master of the house said he was going to bed and told them to do likewise. So the two girls, whose names were Otane and Oharu, readily retired to their rooms. As I mentioned before, by that time it was raining cats and dogs.

Allow me to pause for a moment here to tell you how the Oda house is laid out. It is entirely in the Japanese style, with the master bedroom and a study on the first floor, beneath which there are two open *tatami* rooms. Ōtera was given the room just below the study on that night. A little way down the passageway outside this room stood the maids' quarters and on the outside near the kitchen was another building where the houseboy slept, an ex-sailor named Jinbei.

Now the two sleepy maids had been rubbing their eyes for some time by then and having obtained their master's permission, they went straight to their room, pulled out their futons and immediately fell into the type of sound sleep that is enjoyed by most people in service.

Before long Otane, the elder of the two, woke up. Feeling that she had been asleep for quite some time and also that she had woken up naturally she looked, as she always did, at the alarm clock next to her pillow which had been put there by her employer. It was still only one-thirty. The rain had not let up. Just as the relieved Otane was about to go back to sleep she heard what she thought was someone screaming. And then she heard what sounded like a sliding partition falling over on the first floor.

Otane almost let out a scream herself, but instead she pulled her nightgown tight around herself and huddled under the covers holding her breath. After a few moments she timidly raised her head and once again heard the sound of someone groaning. Overcome with fear, Otane began to pummel Oharu awake, who was sprawled out sleeping next to her. When Oharu heard what had happened she began to tremble and the two of them resolved to wake the houseboy.

In order to accomplish this, however, as you will have gathered from my explanation a moment ago, it was necessary to go outdoors and into the other building – far too daunting a feat for two girls to undertake at such a late hour and in the midst of such a frightful downpour. So they decided instead to go and wake the guest who was staying in the room just down the hall.

The two crept down the hall shivering with fright and stood outside the door to the room where they called out Ōtera's name two or three times. But there was no answer. When they gathered up the courage to slide open the door where they believed Ōtera was sleeping, his bed was as empty as a cast-off snake skin. As they stood dumbfounded in the room they heard the sound of someone falling in the room directly overhead. Shrieking with fear they ran out of the room and went straight to wake the houseboy. A strapping ex-sailor in his forties, the houseboy grabbed a large walking stick, told the maids to sit tight, and stormed up the stairs.

It was then that the scene of the tragedy was witnessed for the first time by an outsider. As Jinbei came upstairs followed by the two frightened maids they were confronted with a horrifying scene.

The Odas' bedroom was at the top of the stairs and the *shōji* screen was open in the middle – actually one whole screen had been ripped out – so that the room's interior was clearly visible. A lamp on a rosewood table in one corner lit the room with a dim light of about five candlepower. The mosquito netting had been ripped off its hooks at two points and stuffed in a corner with the rest of it dangling loosely. Two futons were laid out with their pillows towards the desk. Michiko lay on the futon to the left. She was naked from chest up with a cord like a kimono lashed tightly around her breasts all the way up to her neck. With each groan, bright red blood spilled out from a gash in the vicinity of her full white breasts.

Seizō was half-way out of the other futon, face-down on the table. Michiko seemed almost dead already but Seizō was in the last agonising throes.

It has taken me some time to describe all of this but of course in reality it only took a second for Jinbei and the maids to take all of it in. In fact very little time had passed since Otane first woke up. Seeing what had happened to his master, Jinbei ran to him and held him from behind. His kimono was covered in blood that came flowing out of his mouth and from a wound on his right breast. As Jinbei lifted him up Seizō looked him straight in the eye and said, with all the strength he had left in his body, 'Ōtera... Ōtera...'

Michiko was in a grave condition but her husband's scream seemed to revive her and suddenly she said a single word, 'Ichirō...'

Jinbei and the two maids all heard this quite clearly. It caused them all to catch their breath at once.

As soon as Jinbei heard his master say 'Ōtera' his first thought was to find the man. He looked around him and there, in the adjoining study, he saw a man standing as rigid as a statue. Of course you will have guessed that this was Ōtera. We are told that his pyjamas were covered in blood and all dishevelled as if he had just been in a fight. He held something shiny in his right hand as he stood there silently in the dark, looking like a man deep in meditation.

The courageous Jinbei raised his cane and struck Ōtera repeatedly on the right hand. As soon as the ostensible murder weapon fell out of Ōtera's hand Jinbei tackled him. The latter put up no resistance, almost as if he were expecting it, and in no time Jinbei had tied him up with an undersash. Jinbei ordered the frightened maids to call the police immediately. The investigation began from that point on and I suppose most of you know the rest since the newspapers covered it so extensively, but allow me briefly to remind you of a couple of important points.

III

I learned afterwards that the prosecutor who got wind of the murders immediately requested an arrest warrant from the examining judge who then took care of the autopsies, the inspection of the crime scene and the securing of the weapon. What I am telling you now is based partly on the results of those investigations and part of it was already known to the public at the time. So the order in which I came to know the facts is different from the order in which I am going to relate them to you now. But we won't bother with such matters of legal procedure and I'll just tell you what was going on at the time.

The cause of death of Oda Seizō and his wife Michiko was of course determined to be homicide. The weapon used was an extremely sharp blade. The pool of blood around Seizō was determined to have come from his lungs and the mortal wound to have been a blow to his right breast. He was stabbed through his pyjamas and there was also a bruise on his forehead but this latter was assumed to have been caused when he fell on the table. In other words, Seizō was only wounded in one place.

But Michiko, as I said a moment ago, died a horrible and cruel death. She was wounded in three places: stabbed on each of her breasts and cut across her cheek. The stab wound that killed her was the one on her left breast. The top of her nightgown had been torn off and her hands were tied behind her with her own sash. Her wrists were rubbed raw, presumably from having struggled to untie herself or to keep from being tied up, and the skin on her throat was slightly chafed as well from the cord wrapped around it. It was also established that man and wife had breathed their last within moments of each other.

The culprit was of course Ōtera Ichirō and he was apprehended at the scene of the crime. The object in Ōtera's hand was a jackknife that Oda Seizō kept in his study and it proved to have been the weapon that inflicted the victims' wounds.

Ōtera did not resist arrest but he refused to speak when he was brought to the police. I believe he spent two whole days without uttering a single word.

The prosecutor immediately brought charges against him for the murder of Mr and Mrs Oda.

I was engaged to work on this case by a certain aristocrat who was very close friends with Ōtera. Ōtera, it seems, had a very quiet and prepossessing character. He was also such a beautiful young man that one wished he were a woman. Given his humble circumstances he had a very impressive set of friends, including the aristocrat in question, a great supporter of his who was no doubt quite smitten with his looks and his character. When all of this happened the aristocrat came to me and asked me to do what I could for Ōtera. He said it was inconceivable that Ōtera Ichirō could possibly have committed murder and I resolved to put my services at the young man's disposal.

By the time I took the case on, however, the prosecutor had already filed charges, Ōtera had broken his silence and confessed to the crime, and it was all over the newspapers. I have a copy of one of the newspaper accounts with me here that I would like to read to you.

Suspect Confesses to Murder of Wealthy Couple
A Crime of Passion Reveals the Dark Side of High Society

Ōtera Ichirō (24), who was captured at the scene of the murder of Mr and Mrs Oda Seizō of 'K', finally broke his silence last night and confessed to the crime under intense questioning by the police. The confession not only confirmed that this gentle and attractive youth is in fact a vile murderer but also exposed the utter depravity of domestic life in today's high society.

It was passion that motivated the grisly murder. Passion in the form of a repugnant and adulterous love affair. It seems that the young and beautiful Oda Michiko had been intimately involved for a year with Ōtera. The two had known each other for two years and Michiko, whose husband felt no love for her and whose illness made him dependent on medication, fell in love with the attractive young man after just a few meetings. At first Ōtera took pity on Michiko for her unhappy home life, but then a few sweet words from her caused him to forget his status as a student and become drunk on the sweet wine of adultery. The two became increasingly close and planned frequent trysts, taking advantage of the husband's disinclination to put any restraints on his wife. Their behaviour was disgraceful. On some occasions Michiko would visit Ōtera's lodgings herself, and sometimes they would meet at Tokyo station for a trip to the suburbs. A search of Ichirō's home after his confession turned up more than one hundred letters written to him from Michiko. But Michiko's heart had recently begun to wander and the wanton woman had fallen in love with Ōtera's friend Tomoda Takeshi (the man who had been at 'K' earlier on the evening of the murder). This was the motive behind the murder.

On the evening of the 16th the brazen-faced Michiko played mahjong with her two lovers and her husband, toying with the three men under the guise of the game. When Ōtera happened to overhear her setting a date for a rendezvous with Tomoda he became enraged and lay awake later waiting for an opportunity to confront her and ask her true intentions. When Michiko came downstairs to use the toilet, Ōtera

embraced her and pleaded with her to continue the illicit relation. But Michiko, whose fickle heart had already moved on,
rebuffed him summarily. It was this treatment that resolved
Ōtera to murder the young couple. That night he sneeked into
their room, delivering a serious blow to Seizō while he
abstained from administering mortal blows to the hateful
Michiko so that he could torture her to death...

This article is quite tame compared to most of the press coverage
at the time, which tended to represent the events of that evening
in an even more sensational manner including descriptions of the
love affair of Michiko and Ichirō, all the better to fan the flames
of the readers' curiosity.

But all of the newspapers saw Michiko's tragic death as just
deserts for her shameful conduct and made no bones about
expressing sympathy for Seizō, who had lost not only his wife,
but his life as well. There were even a couple of newspapers that
took the trouble of visiting Michiko's family, the Kawakamis, in
order to claim that however reprehensible the daughter's
conduct had been, the widowed mother who had sacrificed her
daughter for money was no less to blame.

As I mentioned earlier I became involved in this matter after
the prosecutor had brought the indictment and the case had
advanced to the preliminary hearing. As you are all aware at this
point, it was not possible to have any contact with the defendant
and neither the prosecutor nor the judge was sharing any information with me, so I had no other option but to find what information I could on the outside. For this reason, at this stage, all
of my knowledge about the case came solely from the newspapers. Of course I did all that I could on my own. I was able,
for example, to meet with Tomoda, but all I could find out from
him was that the Odas' daily life was as frosty and strained as
the rumours said. As for Michiko, Tomoda categorically denied

any special relationship with her. He also claimed that the story about him having had some sort of secret communication with her on the night of the murder was entirely a fabrication of the newspapers. He did tell me that he had received a number of letters from Michiko some of which were quite upsetting. Once she complained of her husband's cruelty and solicited his sympathy upon showing him fresh bruises on both of her arms. He claimed that this was the extent of their interactions and he seemed not to know much about Michiko's relations with Ōtera. He did say, however, that he believed that Ōtera was very much in love with Michiko.

IV

Of course, the minute they catch a likely suspect the newspapers waste no time in making out that he's the real culprit and their readers have the bad habit of believing them. If he turns out to be innocent, people are just as quick to attack the police and kick up a ruckus about trampling on people's human rights or torture or what have you. The problem starts when people assume that the suspect is the perpetrator. As far as we lawyers are concerned the suspect is not guilty even after the prosecution has indicted him. All the indictment means is that the prosecutor believes the suspect is guilty. Of course the prosecutor needs quite a bit of evidence to make him think so, but we cannot in any circumstances assume guilt until it has been proven in the court of law. Even when the newspapers have pronounced someone guilty there is still plenty of room for doubt and in many instances they have in fact been proven wrong.

As long as the full details of the case had not been released it was of course impossible to know anything for certain, but it did look awfully unlikely that anyone besides Ōtera could possibly have committed the murder.

The only way to find out more information was to wait until the case went to trial. Finally, four months after the murder had taken place the preliminary judge handed the case over to the trial judge. It was at this point that Ōtera Ichirō learned that he was to stand trial for the murder of Oda Seizō and his wife Michiko.

Based on the facts I had heard up until this point was it not time for me to let the matter go? Did it not look as though Ōtera was guilty beyond a shadow of a doubt? I, for one, thought not. Gentlemen as intelligent as you will no doubt also have noticed that even among the facts so far established there were several points that did not add up. It was these doubts that made me decide to undertake the defence of the accused and to do all I could to uncover the truth about this case.

My first doubt had to do with the following.

A reasonable enough motive had been established. Ōtera was angry that Michiko had transferred her affections to Tomoda and when he reproached her with this she brushed him off so cruelly that he conceived the desire to kill her. And yet we know that the knife Ōtera had was not his own but belonged to the victim Oda Seizō.

The intended victim may have been a helpless woman. But her husband was there with her. And however ill he was, he surely would not have watched quietly while his wife was murdered. So anyone who wanted to kill Michiko in that room would have to kill her husband as well. It is also uncertain whether Ōtera knew that there was a jackknife in the room. This would suggest the possibility that Ōtera burst into the room prepared to kill two people with bare hands and empty fists. Under normal circumstance, this would be rather peculiar. Of course Ōtera may not have intended to kill anyone when he came to stay with the Odas. But once he made that decision it is quite likely that he would have taken a towel or something with him, even if he had just five minutes to prepare. At a pinch even an empty cigarette case could work as a murder weapon. Add to this the fact that Ōtera was physically weak and more like a woman than a man and one has to think that, while it may not be impossible, it was certainly highly unlikely that he would have gone into that room unprepared. Clearing this up would make it easier to determine whether there was an intent to kill. And even if it turned out that Ōtera was behind this tragedy it would be to his advantage to have this matter clarified.

My second doubt had to do with the scene of the crime. This was a crucial point.

When someone kills a husband and wife it is typical for them either to kill the man first or to tie him up while they kill or violate the woman. In this case, however, the wife had been stripped from the waist up and her hands were tied behind her back. If what I was told was in fact the case the couple died at almost exactly the same time. So one has to ask what Seizō was doing the whole time while Ōtera was taking his revenge by tying Michiko up, stripping her naked, wounding her on the face and breasts, and finally killing her. And would not Michiko herself have screamed bloody murder? how could it be explained if she hadn't? I wondered what the accused said about all of this, and what sorts of theories the prosecutor and the examining judge had come up with.

There is one more suspicious point I want to mention. This is something that crops up often in the novels you gentlemen write so you might have thought of it already. It's about the fatal wound inflicted on the victim Seizō: a stab wound in the right breast. It's not easy to stab someone in the right breast from head-on unless one is left-handed. This is not a matter just for novels. It is a serious matter in real life as well. It is only possible for a right-handed person to inflict such a wound if the victim is in just the right position so that his chest comes into contact with the assailant's right hand. Now I had not heard that Ōtera was left-handed. So we needed another theory to account for this wound. One might imagine, for example, that the two had been struggling over the knife and Seizō was wounded accident-ally (in this case it would be more natural to assume that Seizō, and not Ōtera, was wielding the weapon). This point is very important because leaving aside the question of Michiko, it has a bearing on whether Ōtera could be charged with the murder of Seizō. If Ōtera were not convicted of murdering Seizō, even if he were found guilty of some other charge, it would have a serious impact on the final verdict. The issue here is not just whether he killed one person or two. To put it simply, if Ōtera did not kill Seizō but did kill Michiko, there is a chance he would get the death penalty. But there is also a chance that he would not. If, on the other hand, Ōtera killed Seizō it would be a case of an adulterer killing the husband. And in such a case, even if he did not kill Michiko, he would certainly receive the death penalty.

They say that Ōtera gave a complete confession. But what exactly did he say? The newspaper article I read to you earlier was obviously too sketchy an account. So I waited impatiently until the day when the details of the interrogation would be made available.

I waited, but not of course idly. Instead I made use of the time to think through a few theories of my own. I'd like to share with you a few scenarios I was considering at the time.

What if the defendant had insisted on his innocence? Was there no theory by which he might be proved not guilty?

I was convinced that such a theory had to exist. Of course detective novelists like you could no doubt come up with all kinds of ideas. But let me tell you about one of mine.

What do you think, for example, about the possibility that it was Oda Seizō himself who murdered his wife? What if we were to hypothesise that Oda Seizō discovered his wife's adultery that night or perhaps he knew already but something that night drove his anger to such a pitch that he killed her?

Let's say that he had been suspicious of his wife's behaviour for some time. On that evening something happened between the two of them and the husband confirmed his wife's infidelity. Michiko shows no inclination to change her ways. Even worse, she sometimes behaves strangely with the two other men. Finally Seizō takes it into his head to kill his wife. But she has betrayed him and it won't be enough just to kill her with a single blow. So he waits until she is asleep, pounces on her and ties her up. He wants to make her suffer as much as possible so he cuts her in the face and on her breast. At this point Ōtera, perhaps having heard the commotion, comes bounding into the room. Of course Seizō is just as angry with Ōtera so he goes for him with the knife as well. But let's say it's Seizō who ends up getting hurt in the struggle. Might we not imagine such a circumstance? If that were the case Ōtera would not be guilty of murdering Michiko and it would be a case of manslaughter or he might even be let off for self-defence vis-à-vis Seizō. In any case, it would not be murder. It sounds a bit too much like a novel to be true, but for a while I considered it in all seriousness.

There are, however, quite a few points that cannot be explained by this theory. First of all, the idea that someone would choose a night when a guest is in the house to murder and torture his wife is highly unlikely. Then there is the fact that Ōtera was sleeping in the room just below the couple's bedroom. It would be hard enough in a western-style house, but even granting that the person downstairs were asleep could you actually take so much time to commit a murder in a Japanese house? Or rather would it ever occur to you that such a thing was possible? Even if we assume that Seizō was carried away by anger how likely is it that he would have decided to torture and murder Michiko on a night like this? Seizō murdering Michiko on the spur of the moment might be different, but one can be sure that he would not have committed such a brutal act without expecting that Ōtera would come upon the scene.

Then there is the problem of Ōtera's arrival into the room at that time, when Michiko was already tied up and wounded. Now this is not impossible to explain if you assume that he ran into the room as soon as he heard Michiko scream. But Michiko must have started to scream from the moment she was tied up. Earlier, I neglected to mention another factor that worked in the favour of the defendant: namely, there was no evidence that Michiko's mouth was gagged.

So here again, we have to wonder what Michiko was doing.

The idea that Seizō died from a wound received as he struggled with Ōtera, while possible, starts to seem rather far-fetched.

It would only be possible if Ōtera were left-handed. The notion that Seizō killed himself after he murdered Michiko seems equally unlikely unless Seizō were also left-handed.

Seizō, however, appears not to have been left-handed. And neither does Ōtera.

As a result, my theory that Ōtera was innocent is back on shaky ground.

All of you have fertile imaginations and I have no doubt that another theory has occurred to you that would explain several of the facts in this case as I have described them thus far. I will not name it here but I imagine that as detective-novel writers you will surely have thought of it.

If this last remaining possibility were true, however, why did Ōtera admit to the murders? Most problematic of all, moreover, were the words the dead couple uttered right before they died. Seizō clearly said 'Ōtera' and Michiko 'Ichirō' before they died. If this was indeed confirmed it was not hard to know what it meant. With only one possible exception, it must have been Michiko calling out the name of her lover as she died. But in any case, the biggest problem was the defendant's confession. There is no more powerful evidence than a confession. And Ōtera Ichirō had made a complete confession.

I went back and forth over it in my mind, thinking that, whatever happened with the murder charge against Michiko, he might end up being charged with manslaughter in Seizō's death. As I continued in this confused state I was on tenterhooks waiting for the final decision of the preliminary trial.

V

The decision for which I had waited so impatiently was finally handed down. As I said earlier, the case was to be moved on to a public trial. In my capacity as the barrister for the defendant Ōtera Ichirō I quickly ordered all of the case records. With what excitement I finally held the documents in my hands! I read through them ravenously from start to finish, as one would read letters from a lover. With eyes sharpened so as almost to penetrate the paper they were written on, I read through them all without missing even a single character.

And yet what did I find there? Having read them all I felt utterly disappointed. I was disappointed to discover that the newspaper reports had been mostly free of inaccuracies. The defendant Ōtera Ichirō had, both to the prosecutor and in the pretrial hearing, admitted his guilt. He had pleaded guilty to the murder of both husband and wife.

The few doubts on which I had pinned my hopes were summarily dispatched by the extreme rationality of the confession. At the same time, it was altogether too passionate a confession for it to be fraudulent. It was too earnest not to be true. And what purpose, after all, could possibly be served by the defendant lying to the prosecutor and the preliminary trial judge?

I have a facsimile here of the record of that interview. Allow me to read it aloud and to show you the exact transcript of the questioning and his responses during the pretrial. (The original is lacking voiced consonant marks and punctuation, but I will try to read it as a normal text to make it easier to understand.)

Q: Does this mean that the defendant resolved to kill Michiko because she had transferred her affections to another man?

A: I decided to kill Michiko because, while she had been quite kind to me up until then, she had treated me coldly after her change of heart and had begun to love Tomoda instead.

Q: Did the defendant know that Michiko was in love with Tomoda?

A: Until that day I had no conclusive proof of it. That evening I became convinced of it based on the way they were speaking to each other.

Q: When did the defendant decide to kill Michiko?

A: It was late at night on that day. Until then I was suffering enormously on the inside but the thought of killing her had never crossed my mind.

Q: Please explain the steps that led you to want to kill her.

A: When we were playing mahjong on that day – it was around nine-thirty I think – Tomoda got up to go to the toilet, after which Michiko left the room as well, looking as if she had something to do in the kitchen. I had been suspicious of their behaviour for some time already and felt something wasn't right, so after a few moments I excused myself as well, saying I needed to use the toilet. I headed towards the bathroom but purposely turned quietly into the dark corridor where I discovered Michiko and Tomoda whispering to each other. I clearly heard Michiko say, 'All right then – six o'clock the day after tomorrow at the usual place.' I couldn't quite make out what Tomoda said in reply but I sensed that the two had grasped each other's hands. I did not actually see this, but I felt it quite clearly.

Q: Tomoda says that he may have gone to the toilet at that time but that he did not speak to Michiko. Why is that?

A: That is an outright lie. I remember the conversation quite clearly. And besides, if I hadn't heard it I would not have become so furious. Overhearing it made me deeply angry. I felt that I had no more hope in the world. At that point, however, I had not yet thought of killing Michiko. That night I ended up staying in the room downstairs and went to bed after midnight, but I was so devastated that I couldn't fall asleep and lay in bed moaning for about an hour. After a while I sensed someone coming downstairs and, listening closely, determined that it was Michiko. After she had gone into the toilet, I thought things over and decided that I had to speak to her and try to change her mind. So when she came out of the toilet I stopped her in the corridor and spoke to her. I said everything I could think of to win back her heart. But she had already given her heart to Tomoda and she showed no signs of returning to me. To make matters worse, she said, 'Have you not been loving me behind Seizō's back until now? You and I are both adulterers, aren't we? What right does an adulterer like you have to tell me whom I can or cannot love? My husband might have a right to complain but I fail to see why I should listen to you.' Of course I knew I had no rights in the matter but her way of putting it was so harsh that I said two or three things in my defence, to which she replied, 'Do you actually think I cared about you? What a silly boy you are! I went with you just to tease you, you know. Now if you don't stop this whining this instant I'm going to have to wake up Seizō. Let me go now, if you please!' So saying, she turned her back on me and vanished back up the stairs.

All I could do was go back to bed. But as I thought about how horribly rude she had been and – although of course I am in no position to judge – how disgraceful and wanton her behaviour had been for a married woman, I could hardly stand it and resolved to kill her and then to kill myself. I had lived my life for her up until that point and now that I had lost her I saw no reason to go on living.

Q: *Where did the defendant intend to kill Michiko?*

A: *I planned to go into her bedroom and kill her.*

Q: *Were you aware that her husband was sleeping in Michiko's room?*

A: *Yes, I knew.*

Q: *Did the defendant believe that he could kill Michiko quietly while her husband was sleeping?*

A: *No. I knew that, if I killed Michiko, Seizō was sure to wake up.*

Q: *So what did you plan to do when Seizō woke up?*

A: *At first I thought if he woke up when I killed her I would come clean and confess my crime and then kill myself. But depending on Seizō's attitude I was prepared to kill him as well.*

Q: *Did the defendant harbour ill feelings towards Seizō?*

A: *I had always hated him for mistreating the woman I loved. But what bothered me most was simply the fact that he was married to her. His existence was hateful to me. This may be hard for you to understand but it is true.*

Q: Did you attempt to use a weapon of some sort in order to kill them?

A: I looked around for something but couldn't find anything.

Q: By what method did you plan to kill them?

A: At the time I was quite delirious so I did not really think it through but my plan was to barge into the room and strangle Michiko as she slept with my bare hands. As for Seizō, he was ill so I figured one good blow to the head would be enough to finish him off.

Q: Describe the way in which you killed them.

A: After I had determined that they were both asleep I quietly drew back the shōji *and entered the room. I then mounted Michiko like a horse as she slept inside the mosquito net and immediately proceeded to close my hands around her neck. At this point Seizō woke up and called out, 'Who's there?' There was no way around it so I spoke as I had planned.*

'I have wronged you terribly. Please forgive me. I must apologise.'

As I said this, Seizō sat up on the floor and said, 'What? You're Ōtera aren't you? What on earth are you doing in our bedroom at this hour?' To which I replied, 'I came here in order to kill Michiko-san and ready to die myself. I don't know how much you know, but the truth is that Michiko-san and I have been committing adultery for quite some time now. Michiko doesn't love you. And you don't love her either, do you? I am Michiko's true lover. It is I who possess her. But she has betrayed me and I am here now to punish her.'

Q: Was Michiko listening to this without saying anything?

A: When she first opened her eyes she was trembling with shock but once I started talking she called me a liar, 'a filthy no-good liar'. But she did not scream or call for help. She was too busy trying to justify herself to her husband.

Q: Describe what happened after that.

A: If Seizō had listened even a little to what I was saying I might have been able to avoid killing him. But despite my full and honest confession, he refused to listen. Indeed, rather than listening at some point he grabbed a knife that must have been on the desk and came after me with it all pale and trembling. His face looked to me like the face of a devil. I flew into a rage, tightened my fists and punched him in the head. He let out a short grunt, fell over, and hit his head hard on the corner of the desk. He looked like he had spit up blood at the same time that he fell over and he immediately lost consciousness. The mosquito net had come undone during the scuffle and was fluttering around so I kicked it violently out of the way. Michiko screamed when her husband fell over and ran over to him and tried to embrace him. I immediately pulled her by the hair and held Seizō's knife to her neck and told her I would kill her if she made a sound. But she looked like she was going to scream anyway so I cut her on the face. Just as she started to scream she fainted and collapsed. Looking at this woman whom I had so loved until then, in nothing but her nightgown with a cut across her face, I was overcome by a wave of cold-blooded cruelty. I knew I would not be satisfied if I killed her with one blow so I decided to torment her first. Taking advantage of the fact that she had fainted I quickly untied the sash around her waist and bound her with it. Then I stabbed her in the right breast, avoiding her vital organs. I was not concerned for my own safety at the time but I planned to kill her immediately and then kill myself if anyone came into the room.

Michiko started breathing heavily because of the pain. I decided I didn't want her making any noise and pressed her face down onto my lap. As she lay there deprived of her freedom and groaning in agony I showered her with every curse imaginable. She seemed to be suffering terribly, but Seizō had meanwhile regained consciousness and seemed to be moving about so I pointed the knife towards the location of her heart and finished her off with a single powerful thrust.

Seizō was trying to get up and get his breath back so I forced his head down onto my lap as well and stabbed him in the chest.

Just then I heard footsteps coming up the stairs, so I hurriedly stood up and as I was vacillating over whether to kill myself with the knife Seizō, who had not yet died, tried to get up again. That was when the houseboy came in and cradled Seizō in his arms.

etc., etc.

This was the gist of Ōtera Ichirō's statement in the preliminary trial, which he stated as well in the presence of the prosecutor.

The preliminary trial judge also questioned Tomoda Takeshi, the houseboy Jinbei, as well as Otane and Oharu. In Tomoda's testimony, as the judge quotes in the document I just read, he categorically denied any physical relationship with Michiko and also denied that he engaged in any whispered conversation with her on the night in question. He does, however, admit to having carried on a correspondence with her by letter.

As for Jinbei, Otane, and Oharu's testimonies, they of course focused primarily on descriptions of the crime scene.

The judge focused most closely on the dying words spoken by Seizō and his wife. When he was asked about this, Jinbei responded with the following.

As I said a minute ago, when I tried to hold the boss in my arms he was already almost dead. I kept saying, 'Boss! Boss!' and his eyes opened just barely and then all of a sudden he said, in a surprisingly loud voice, 'Ōtera… It's Ōtera.'

He said it really loud so there was no mistaking it. He knew it was me at the time so I'm sure it was a message meant for me.

We thought Mrs Oda was already a goner but when she heard the boss say that she started to say something herself. Otane and I ran over to her and she opened her eyes too. She looked right at me and said '… Ichirō…'

Just that one word. Her voice was faint but I heard it clearly. And she didn't say it crazy like. It was like you say someone's name when they just came for a visit, not like she was calling out his name.

Otane gave a similar account.

As you have all surmised by now, everything I wanted to know was clarified by this in a most unfortunate way. My theory putting responsibility for the murder on the husband crumbled in the face of this testimony.

My doubts had disappeared for the moment. Even worse, as if to further validate the defendant's confession, a large number of letters Michiko had written to him turned up at his residence. It must be said that these letters did not contain any passionate declarations of love and therefore did not constitute any direct proof of adultery or demonstrate conclusively that the tragedy had occurred as a result of such, but there was no denying their value as indirect evidence.

Once the case had moved on from the pretrial stage I was allowed for the first time to meet the defendant as his lawyer. My first impression on meeting him was one of astonishment at his beauty. Little wonder, I thought, that Michiko had chosen him as her lover. His health did not seem to have suffered much by his incarceration; he was full of energy and fairly exuded the beauty of youth. I am a man who is quite capable of appreciating a good-looking youth, but seeing Ōtera I felt this particularly deeply. Despite all of the facts that I had gathered so far, I felt that this man could not possibly have committed such a crime. As a man of the law I knew very well that faces can be deceptive – indeed that the most heinous crimes are sometimes committed by persons who don't appear capable of harming a fly – and yet I still found myself inexplicably drawn to this young man.

I spoke to him first of the aristocrat who had engaged me on his behalf and told him that for that person's sake he should be as forthcoming as possible. Then I spoke to him of my own predisposition in his favour and strongly urged him to be honest with me. Finally, I endeavoured to ascertain as much detail from him as the limits of the law would permit.

He raised his beautiful eyebrows and pronounced himself profoundly grateful towards the aristocrat and me but at the same time asked us please not to place any hopes on his case. He spoke of many sad things, saying that he was already resigned to any and every outcome and that we should not worry about him since, even should he take this dishonour with him to the grave, he had no parents to be saddened by it.

I still remember the last day I saw him. A gentle rain was falling. Glancing from time to time with those beautiful eyes towards the sky he said sadly, 'I am prepared, so please don't worry about me. I… have already given up.' As he said goodbye and I took my leave of him I was assailed by a wave of unspeakable loneliness and tottered home in the rain on foot, somehow unable to call a cab.

Strangely, however, I was still unable to abandon my hopes. I took every opportunity to question Tomoda, Jinbei, and the others but these efforts yielded nothing and the days flew by in vain until all that remained was to await the defendant's testimony in court.

It was true that Ōtera had confessed everything to the prosecutor and in the pretrial, but the public trial still remained. According to the laws of our country, the public trial mattered most. The defendant might have had some reason to proclaim his guilt up until now. It was still possible that in the public trial he might overturn his previous confession and deliver a different testimony altogether. Such things do happen from time to time as I am sure you gentlemen are all aware.

Thus while it might seem overly pertinacious of me, I still clung to this public trial as a last hope. I believe I can count on you all to grasp fully the difficulty of my position as his lawyer.

The public trial finally began. Since all the newspapers covered the trial you are probably all familiar with it already so I will not go into any detail here.

My last hope was dashed. The defendant wasted no time in admitting to the crime in this venue as well. Not only did he admit his guilt, he succeeded in moving the hearts of an entire courtroom full of listeners with the passionate and tearful confession of his tortured love for Michiko, told with all the feeling of a mind overtaken by a monstrous love and the fearsome monomania of youth. Of course there were surely some among his listeners who crinkled their brows in scepticism, unable to overlook his unpardonable crime and its reprehensible motive. But I believe that there were also those who, knowing what it is to be young and in love, were able to feel some measure of compassion for this unfortunate young man.

Foolishly – and yes I do mean foolishly – our young man did not stop at admitting his guilt in the crime but also stated that he still hated Michiko. He even intimated that if she came back to life and spoke those same words to him that he would murder her a dozen or even a hundred times all over again.

In other words, it did not appear that the defendant was experiencing any remorse over having killed Michiko or even for having done away with Seizō.

Given that the defendant, whom I had made every effort to protect, was stating all of this in court without hesitation and, to borrow the words of the prosecutor's closing argument, with an 'incomparably brazen and shameless attitude', my position as his defence barrister was pathetic indeed.

But despite all of that, I continued to do what I could for him. I requested that the court permit me to call as witnesses Tomoda Takeshi, Jinbei, Otane and Oharu.

My last desperate efforts were focused on the words that the Odas had spoken as they died. In the end, Jinbei was the only witness who was called but unfortunately with no positive effect. In his testimony Jinbei only repeated what he said at the pretrial. With the consent of the chief judge I asked the witness directly if he believed that Michiko was calling to her lover, but Jinbei insisted that she seemed to be saying Ichirō's name to herself.

I then shifted the emphasis to the question of why Michiko would have used his first name 'Ichirō' rather than his family name 'Ōtera', but Jinbei clearly stated that she was in the habit of calling him 'Ichirō' rather than 'Ōtera -san'. After this I did not pursue the matter further.

There was no longer even a single point of doubt. All of the witnesses' testimonies suggested that Ōtera Ichirō was the murderer. And the most damning evidence of all was the defendant's own confession. As I stated earlier, I had hoped that the defendant might overturn his earlier confession in the public trial, but the result was instead as I have described it.

I, of course, have no experience as a policeman, nor as a prosecutor or a judge, so I know very little of the internal procedures of crime investigations. One does often hear that the police have a tendency to extract confessions at times by force and violence. But no matter how much I might oppose them, I do believe that defendants are treated reasonably well by the prosecutor's office and during the pretrial process. In the case of public trials everything is open to public scrutiny and this is even more true. For these reasons it was clear to me that the defendant in this case had not made his confession under duress.

I am of course aware that defendants have been known intentionally to make false confessions. You gentlemen are no doubt also aware of this. This tends to happen in the following cases.

In some instances, defendants do this in order to attain notoriety.

Human beings never seem to lose their love for the theatrical, and it sometimes happens that people confess to serious crimes in order to shock the public and make themselves famous. But they rarely wish to sacrifice their lives for such fame and often end up retracting their confession in court. They are also usually aware that the facts will overturn them once they get to court.

Many of these criminals have committed other petty crimes or, when that is not the case, have committed another crime the gravity of which has already placed them at serious risk of the death penalty. As for Ōtera Ichirō, however, he had not committed any other crimes and he was too well educated to have done it simply for the notoriety it would gain him. For these reasons it seemed unlikely that he would number among this category of criminals.

In other cases, criminals will use a false confession of a minor crime in order to cover up a more serious one. By ensuring that they are imprisoned for the minor crime they hope to avoid prosecution for the major one. Of course the crime to be covered up in these cases tends to be many times more serious than the crime that is falsely confessed to. But since the crime that Ōtera Ichirō was confessing to was itself already a major one, it was unlikely that he was doing so in order to conceal another.

There are also other cases, often met with in detective fiction, especially French detective fiction, in which the defendants sacrifice themselves in order to protect a lover who is the true guilty party. It is actually more common for women to do this than men. But what about Ōtera Ichirō? In this case it is clear that no one entered the Oda home from outside and Jinbei and the two maids could not possibly have committed the murders. Even if Ōtera was in love with one of the maids and she had done it, it would have been impossible for him to cover up the crime. There does not appear to be another criminal here for whom he might be covering. It is also unlikely that he was trying to protect the reputation of the woman he loved. Indeed, far from protecting her, as I have explained at length already, he continued to abuse the woman he loved even in death in his confession until not an inch of her remained unblemished.

In light of all of this it is exceedingly unlikely that Ōtera Ichirō's confession was untrue. The logic and precision of his statements, moreover, made it unlikely that he was suffering from some form of delusion. (The court was particularly careful to establish the state of his mental health.)

So the public trial proceeded without any further complications and the inquiry was brought to a close. The prosecutor moved to his closing argument, which was just as clear cut as everyone anticipated it would be. After noting how clear the facts in the case were, he castigated the defendant for his 'brazen and shameless attitude' in not only having committed such a crime but in feeling no remorse for it and then asked the judge for the harshest penalty the law would allow. How feeble was the defence I mounted against the prosecutor's accusations! I have never considered myself particularly eloquent but I believe that was the most pathetic performance I have ever given in court. All I could say was to emphasise the defendant's youth and argue that his crime was that of a young man spurred by the anger of the moment. The defendant listened calmly and quietly to the prosecutor's arguments and my own, never once losing the composure of his beautiful face.

Then the day for the reading of the verdict arrived.

As you all know, the verdict called for the death penalty. I knew this the moment I realised that the chief judge had reversed the order of the judgment by reading the facts and reasoning first. The beautiful defendant listened to it being read without showing the slightest sign of surprise.

Once the death penalty had been handed down I made one last effort to convince him to file for an appeal, but the defendant rejected this out of hand. As you are probably aware the penalty was carried out one day this spring and Ōtera Ichirō ended his young life atop the gallows.

The case about which I wanted to tell you was just as I have related it.

After Ōtera died, however, I unexpectedly came into possession of a manuscript that he had written in jail. It is his last will and testament. Since they are irrelevant to the story, I will spare you the details of how exactly I obtained the manuscript.

As soon as I received the manuscript I read it from start to finish without even pausing for breath. What a frightful testament it was! Until now, I have not shown it to anyone else. Allow me to share it with you now. I do so because I believe that the defendant himself would have wanted it to be read in your presence. Without this document, moreover, nothing I have told you up until now has any meaning.

In the manuscript, Ōtera uses various words for 'I', including the formal *watakushi*, the casual and masculine *ore*, and the neutral *jibun*. These choices seem to reflect in each instance his changing mood as he sat in prison.

VI

It was just as I expected.

The verdict called for the death penalty. My ignorant lawyer keeps telling me to appeal. But why would I ever do that? If I were going to appeal now I would have told the truth from the beginning. There would have been no need for me to perpetrate the enormous lie that I worked so hard to concoct during that day in the police headquarters.

Now I will lose my life when the court decides.

Having thrown away my life and my honour, what have I to gain? That hateful, hateful and yet dear, dear Michiko. Oh, Michiko! So many memories, Michiko. I wagered my life on our love. My life, my everything! It was all you, Michiko.

How you teased and toyed with me! Yes – you plucked out my young heart, set it aflame with love and then proceeded to have your way with it.

But now you're a corpse and you have no power over me. What a pitiable woman you are now.

The moment your gorgeous flesh was tied up and died in agony you belonged to me and me alone. Yes – the world believes that you were mine. As long as people remember this story, your name will forever be celebrated along with mine.

Yes, your body might lie next to your husband's. But you – the real you – are here with me. You're with me behind your husband's back. Unfaithful wife! Adulteress! The brand is burned forever into your brow and you must suffer in hell with me forever. What bounteous joy that brings!

Now that I have lost you, o hateful and dear one, how could I possibly live on? What point is there in holding on for years like a living corpse? In any case, I have the same disease as your husband. I am not a well man. It is clear what would happen if I tried to live in society.

Is it so strange that I should want to die now that I have lost you? Besides, I stand to gain something great by dying in the right way. Along with my loss of honour, I am about to gain something far more desirable. I am about to make you into my permanent possession, you on whom I couldn't lay even a finger while I was living.

Yes! And at the same time I will show all the solemn-faced lawyers of the world – including the poor bastard who tried so hard to save me – the true powerlessness of the law that they depend on as if it were a fortress of steel.

How they scurry around, going on and on about evidence! Evidence! Without it, injustice cannot be punished! But the moment they find something that looks like evidence they don't hesitate to send any number of people to their deaths. I wonder if they can possibly understand the fantastic script I have put together for them?

Listen lawyers! I'm going to tell the truth now.

You have condemned an innocent man to death. I am not guilty in the least. Why, then, did I confess?

One reason was to gain eternal possession of the beautiful woman whom I loved more than life and whom I was unable even to touch in this world. Another was to take eternal revenge on the hateful witch who toyed with my pure heart. The third motive was to make use of the legal system in order to rid myself of a life not worth living. And finally, by doing so, I meant to show all of you just how much your confidence in the law is worth.

My father died out of sheer anger over the loss of a mere hundred yen. He was well and truly conned by a certain scoundrel. He was clearly a victim of fraud but lost in court due to the other party's superior knowledge of the law. When, having failed to get his money back, he set out to exact payment from the swindler in the form of blows, it was he who ended up somehow slapped with the charge of slander. This was more than my father could stand. Whether it was a hundred or a thousand yen, it was not about the money. My father had believed in the system. He was convinced that the authorities did not make mistakes. And how did that work out? The system that he had believed in, like a god, refused to take up his case, saying he did not have enough evidence. But while he was unable to get an indictment against the man who had swindled him, he himself was subjected to serious investigation on the charge of slander. For someone who had trusted in the law like my father, this was of course painful to endure. The dishonour of it was unbearable.

As I sit here in my prison cell I can still picture the steady transformation of my father's features as he slipped further each day into depression.

My father's health worsened every day as a result of these affairs and in the end he died – all the while shrieking curses, that the legal system be damned, to the wife and child he left behind.

Oh, how I remember those words. The law be damned! Damn the legal system and its hypocritical standards. I curse the law. As long as the law exists in this world, I curse it. It claims to exist for the sake of justice. It brags that it is on the side of the truth. But how many laws have been made to serve the cause of iniquity! And how powerfully, how tyrannically, has iniquity yoked the law to its purpose!

The time allotted to me is short. I must complete this manuscript as soon as possible. Let me hasten to record the facts.

I met Michiko for the first time on an autumn day three years ago. My mother had uttered her final curse at the world and followed my father in death around the time I graduated from secondary school in my home town and I had been sent to Tokyo to continue my education under the care of my uncle.

Because this uncle had once studied with Michiko's father, who was a university professor, I visited Michiko's house not long after I arrived in Tokyo.

From the first time I met Mrs Kawakami and her daughter I fell in love with Michiko. She was so much more approachable than her mother. How she welcomed me, who had only just arrived from the country, into her home.

Of course Michiko was a proper young lady then.

If there is such a thing in this world as love at first sight, then surely that is what I experienced with Michiko. From the first time I saw her and with the first words we spoke, I was smitten.

She responded with a warm intimacy and I became a frequent visitor at her home even after I had found my own lodgings in a boarding house. Beginning that autumn, this young man from the country lived entirely for Michiko.

As our interactions increased I discovered that she was surrounded by quite a number of admirers. Among her visitors there were even several from the same university I attended. Surrounded by so many men, Michiko was never at a loss, and she managed these interactions with exquisite tact and social poise. For this reason it was impossible to determine whom she liked best. Idiot that I was, I trusted what her mother said, and believed that she held me in special esteem.

Michiko, for her part, scrupulously avoided any serious communication. She was like this with everyone I think. She spoke to all of us about music, literature and theatre, and seemed to enjoy teaching us how to play bridge and mahjong.

During all of this I was quietly in love with her. I was young. Actually I am still young. But when I first met Michiko I was even younger. Still a child really. There was nothing strange about a young man with such pure feelings loving her with all of his being. But if one thinks about it, Michiko's attitude was also responsible for nurturing my obsession with her.

But I confess. I did not feel confident that I would be chosen from among all those men to be her husband. Yet like all people in the throes of love I combined an extreme humility with the most outlandish hopes. For this reason, when I heard that Michiko was to marry Oda Seizō I was in no way surprised, but this did not prevent me from feeling that I had been forced to swallow boiling water. I suffered greatly. I can still remember it – on the night of her wedding (I was invited to the reception but how could I possibly stand the sight of her as a bride?), I didn't know what to do with myself and wandered around Tokyo, going from one bar to another. In the end I passed out drunk in a filthy house somewhere in the alleys of Asakusa, putting an ugly end to a wretched evening.

Michiko was now Mrs Oda, but she still continued to see me. At first I was determined not to see her any more, but when letters from her kept arriving my resolve faltered and our meetings brought me a potent combination of suffering and happiness.

Michiko began to reveal her affection for me only after her marriage. She wrote to me often. Of course these letters did not contain any explicit declarations of her feelings, but to a sensitive young man in love they left a much stronger impression than any conventional love letter stringing together half-baked protestations of love. Michiko had a real gift for writing this kind of letter. Idiot that I was, I kept them with me always and even caressed them as I slept. She was particularly good at writing postscripts and could skilfully pack thousands of words worth of feeling into a two- or three-line 'P.S.'. Before long I had made it a habit to skip straight to the postscript before I even looked at the main body of the letter.

Towards the end of the year two years ago she would come to visit me every time she left 'K' and we would go out for a walk in the Ginza. She never said much during these walks.

For my part, I kept the feeling of being in love with another man's wife tightly wrapped in the sentimentalism of youth and remained silent, hoping my feelings would somehow reach her by osmosis.

When I think back on it now I marvel at how pretentious I was. I had purchased the Reklam edition of *The Sorrows of Young Werther* and carried it with me everywhere in my pocket. With my beginner's German I couldn't read a word of it but I would open it from time to time and let out a sigh.

Oh how the Werther of those days curses his Lotte now!

One evening, as we walked through a certain neighbourhood in Tokyo Michiko said the following to me.

'I love people like you Ichirō. Really I do. How lucky the woman will be who marries you!'

In my mind I cried out, 'It's too late! Why didn't you tell me this sooner?', having interpreted her words in a truly stupid fashion. But how else were these unexpected and craftily formulated words to resonate in the mind of the young man that I was?

There was also the following incident.

I had been invited to play bridge at a friend's home and Michiko was also there. At around five o'clock she said, 'It's time for me to go,' and stood up from her chair.

I was ready to go myself and as I was saying so to our host and about to get up, Michiko interrupted me midsentence and said, looking straight at me, 'I don't mind taking Ichirō with me but lots of people are watching today so maybe that's not such a good idea.'

Being told this in front of so many people, all I could do was stand there in silence, blushing furiously. I had not asked to go with Michiko in her car.

But I couldn't understand if these words of hers were meant as a joke or whether she was serious.

She only began to speak to me seriously about six months before the incident.

It was a conversation on a winter night at the beginning of last year that I once remembered with a sweet yearning but that I now recall with bitterness and extreme discomfort.

On that day Michiko had called me from the Ginza saying she had just come to Tokyo. We went to see a moving picture and afterwards had tea on the first floor of a cafe. Perhaps moved by the unhappy family in the film we'd seen, she said to me, 'Ichirō, do I seem happy?'

'Well…'

I am not very eloquent in situations like these and as I struggled over what to say she said, with a coquettish look in her eyes, 'Well I'm not. I'm not happy actually. Seizō is so mean to me. My husband doesn't love me.'

I had of course heard rumours that Seizō didn't love her. But this was the first time I had heard her complain of it herself.

'But is that really such a problem? At least Seizō doesn't play around with other women behind your back.' I finally managed to produce these words.

'But that's not enough for a woman! What about you Ichirō-san? If you were my husband you wouldn't act like Seizō does, would you?'

I felt my heart leap up into my chest. It was beating furiously. I felt like that ancient Spartan youth with the stolen fox hidden beneath his cloak, allowing it to devour his heart rather than risk discovery. All I could say was, 'Well…' and gaze silently into her eyes. I was entranced by my own amorous suffering. What a fool I was!

I gave her a look of passion and our gazes locked. She looked back, her eyes also aflame, and said, 'Look at this.'

And without giving me a chance to avert my gaze she pulled up her left sleeve and thrust her bare arm in front of my eyes.

The smell of her made me woozy at first, but then I saw a set of snake-like scars that seemed to have been burned into both of her arms.

For a moment we both sat there in complete silence.

'Did Seizō do this to you?' I said unthinkingly, immediately reaching out with my right hand to touch Michiko's plump arm. She did not retract it, and silently nodded while offering it for my inspection.

Oh, you devil! How could you abuse this goddess of a woman? You are not fit to be her husband – nay, not even to be her manservant!

I cursed Seizō's very existence. I railed against him. I cursed her marriage.

In fact I did not go quite that far, but I was in such a state of agitation that I made no bones about my anger at Seizō.

Michiko merely listened in silence and nodded, and when I had finished she said, 'You're the only one I've told so please keep this to yourself.'

Michiko! *You* were the despicable one! When I think now that you played this trick not just on me but on so many other men as well it makes the blood course backwards through my veins!

From that day on I resolved to defend her from the devil who tortured her. I would fight for her no matter what. I was her slave. What a fool I was!

Now Seizō was not all that happy about the freedom he had given Michiko. Apparently he made Michiko suffer for the time she spent with other men like me. Even Seizō, it seemed, could be jealous. But his cool self-regard prevented him from ever addressing this with Michiko directly. Once I had understood this I began to copy Michiko's behaviour towards him. I would purposely say things in his presence to make him uncomfortable. I found pleasure in thus making him miserable. In this way beginning in the spring of last year I met Seizō quite often and relished his unhappiness on each occasion.

On that day, the 18th of August, that accursed day, Seizō's unhappiness was very much in evidence!

I don't know for sure how Michiko was treating Tomoda. But considering that Seizō was being much friendlier to Tomoda than to myself, I assume that he, Tomoda, had not become as close to her as I had.

And yet I cannot be sure of this since Seizō was the kind of man whose attitude often expressed the reverse of his true feelings.

I was not actually invited on that day but, having nothing else to do, had gone there of my own accord. Tomoda happened to be there as well so we began a game of mahjong in the evening.

During this game I was awash with sentimental emotions – on the one hand I was happy to be able to spend so much time with my lover, and on the other I felt sorry for myself for having fallen in love with a married woman and being forced to extract as much pleasure as I could from this silly game.

Once the storm picked up outside I knew I was stuck there for the night and so devoted myself all the more single-mindedly to the mahjong while indulging myself fully in this potent lover's mixture of joy and sadness.

After eight rounds it was still not clear who was winning. It was in the 'west wind' hand that Michiko suddenly did very well.

Or rather someone arranged it so that she did very well. Seizō was the dealer for that hand. I was next to Seizō and just across from Michiko.

It was the eighth and last round and no one had yet made any big wins or losses. The 'prevailing wind' was west when Michiko put together an excellent hand.

Or perhaps it would be better to say that circumstances conspired in such a way that she got a good hand. Seizō was the dealer at the time. I was to Seizō's left and opposite Michiko. After we had gone around four times, Michiko discarded a four and a five character. Then she put down a one and a three dots, followed by one of her south wind tiles. By this time we had discarded quite a few honor tiles and although Michiko was playing a concealed hand she had not given away any of her bamboos, so it was obvious to everyone that she was trying for a full bamboo flush. No one among the other three of us had a ready hand. Seizō, being the dealer, looked particularly vexed and seemed to be in a hurry to finish the round. But he wasn't having much luck, especially with Michiko hanging on to all of her bamboos, making it hard for him to get rid of his. Then it was time for Michiko to pick a tile from the wall. She had lined up all fourteen of her tiles on their sides, with no exposed melds. After thinking for a moment, she discarded a seven bamboo.

'She's got extra,' Seizō mumbled to himself, half out of what seemed genuine anxiety and half to warn the other two of us.

After Tomoda it was my turn. Luckily or not, I drew a three bamboo, the only tile that completed the one-two-three series I was waiting for. All I needed to do then was to discard a superfluous eight bamboo that would leave me with a perfect no-point hand that could go out on either the one, four or seven dots.

In most cases when someone has thrown out a seven bamboo and looks like they are waiting for only one more tile it is risky to discard the eight bamboo. This was all the more true in this case since Michiko was going for a full bamboo flush with a concealed hand using only tiles that she had drawn herself. This was clearly a situation where the general rule that it is better to discard higher numbers did not apply. The eight bamboo that I held in my hand was unquestionably a dangerous tile to discard.

And yet it was my beloved Michiko who sat across from me and the dealer was my nemesis Seizō. Figuring I had three chances to complete my dots *chow*, I went ahead and discarded the eight bamboo and Michiko got her full flush. I will never forget the sour look on Seizō's face at that moment. Michiko was sure to win now but he refused to give up. The result was that we ended up playing four extra rounds.

In the last and final round of this match something else happened to make Seizō unhappy.

It was at the very end of the last, north wind round. Seizō was the dealer and I was next to him again but this time Tomoda was sitting opposite me. I had been pretty unlucky up until that point but suddenly things started to go my way. I was dealt a fantastic set of tiles.

After we had gone around twice, Seizō discarded the north wind tile. I ponged it of course, since north was both the prevailing wind for the round and my seat wind. Then I ponged the green dragon Tomoda played and when he played the nine character I ponged that as well. This made all of the terminals and honours possible limit wins for me as well as the whole character suit.

At this point I was waiting for a four or a seven character, but since no one wanted to discard a character tile and risk paying me the bet by themselves I had no choice but to choose a winning tile from the wall.

It was at this moment that Michiko, who was to my left, mistakenly knocked over two of her tiles. They were both east winds and both limit-winning tiles for me.

'Oh shoot! You saw them didn't you!' she said, as she picked them back up again.

Looking in my direction, Seizō said, 'So that's where they were! I guess you weren't waiting for an east wind after all.'

As he said this, he showed me an east wind from his own hand. He was in the east position but he was having trouble getting rid of it. Michiko did not seem to sense the danger and, saying, 'I guess I'll get rid of them since you saw them,' she inexplicably discarded one of her two east winds. It was my turn to pick from the wall next. And what do you know? – I drew the last east wind. I immediately changed strategy to wait for the east wind and discarded a seven character. Seizō, not noticing that my hand had changed, or perhaps simply thinking it was very unlikely that I had drawn the last east wind, thought he was completely safe and discarded his last east wind. I won handily. And Seizō had to pay me the entire score by himself since he had discarded the winning tile.

He was clearly angry about it, and said to me, 'Why didn't you play that when Michiko discarded her east winds? Didn't you want to win off her?'

I told him that I had only just drawn the east wind and that's why I had only played it when he discarded his, but he clearly didn't believe me.

'Never seen anything like it,' he burst out, and the mahjong game was over. I don't know what Michiko thought of my excuse, but she looked over at me and smiled. She seemed convinced that I had purposely refrained from winning using her tiles.

In this way, that stormy evening wore on with all of us in a strange mood.

I ended up sleeping in a futon they put out for me in the downstairs room.

I spent a lot of time with Seizō but we had never had such unpleasant words as we did that night. It was somehow intensely pleasurable for me but at the same time I had a feeling of unspeakable foreboding as well.

Where would I end up? What was I doing loving another man's wife? I can hear the voices whispering now.

VII

Seizō and Michiko were sleeping in the room just above me. I had never before slept under the same roof as Michiko. This was the first time.

The woman I loved more than my life was another man's wife. The couple were asleep in the same room just above mine. This thought alone was enough to keep me from being able to sleep.

At first I thought the fatigue from having bathed in the ocean that day might be enough to put me to sleep. But then my head filled with thoughts and sleep eluded me. The storm outside had subsided but the rain still fell steadily.

With a youthful sentimentalism I thought about how Michiko and I loved each other but there was nothing we could do about it. I thought of Werther again and gave myself up to a succession of pleasantly sad thoughts. But then my thoughts came back to reality. I shuddered with disgust at the thought of Michiko's voluptuous body sleeping in that room above me with a man who had neither love nor understanding for her. Once again, I cursed Seizō inwardly. I cursed his existence. I listened intently for any sounds as my mind filled with shameful thoughts. The rain did not let up.

A maid could be heard snoring in the other room. As I lay there I alternated between writhing on the floor with all my might just as I had swum in the ocean that day– barely able to resist the impulse to cry out – and shedding tears of romantic, dream-like downheartedness.

For more than an hour I shuttled in this way between heaven and earth as this jumble of feelings mixed with the day's fatigue.

And then, suddenly, I heard the sound of a voice. It was a very quiet sound but my ears were on alert and they told me clearly that it was a human voice.

I sat up halfway and listened with my entire body. There it was again. Then I distinguished the sound of someone quietly moaning. It was coming from the first floor!

I felt my body begin to tremble.

The situation reminded me of a time when as a boy I visited an uncle in the village where I had grown up and overheard my uncle and aunt in their bedroom. Shaking with my own wretchedness I covered my head in the blanket.

After a few moments I ventured out again and heard the sound of someone talking. I got out of bed completely and focused on the room upstairs but this time I was assailed by a strange feeling.

This was clearly different from what I had overheard as a child. As I listened more, I realised just how different it was.

Seizō was scolding her about something. His voice was quiet but seemed angry.

I held my breath and listened. I heard my own name, 'Ōtera'. Then I heard a groaning voice that seemed to belong to Michiko.

There was no longer any doubting it. Seizō suspected something between Michiko and me. Michiko was being made to suffer because of me. I stood up quietly but quickly. My feelings at that time were those of a medieval knight. I went up to the first floor as if I were going to save a damsel in distress.

It is of course a shameful thing to stand outside the doorway of a married couple's bedroom and listen to what is going on inside. But my feelings at that time were of such a nature as to sanctify everything I did. I was going to save an innocent suffering woman. This is what I told myself as I tried to ascertain what was going on in that room.

It was a warm summer night but the *shōji* facing the passageway was closed. I noticed, however, that one could still see inside through a gap at the edge of the *shōji*. I quickly approached it and peered through the gap at the interior of the room.

The floor lamp was clearly visible. By its light, and through the white mosquito netting, I could also clearly see that Seizō was standing there, slightly hunched forward, and crouching down. As I watched he said, 'You love Ōtera, don't you!' in a low, mumbling voice.

I opened the *shōji* a little more so that I could see in front of where Seizō was crouching. I was on the point of opening my mouth to scream.

My beloved Michiko lay there on the floor, her upper body completely naked and her hands tied behind her back. Seizō was abusing her every time he said 'Ōtera' and she was emitting a quiet groan.

I couldn't stand it anymore. Michiko was suffering because of me. I thought of kicking in the *shōji* and barging into the room. But I hesitated for a moment in order to hear what she was saying back to him.

It was all I could do to restrain myself when, at that instant, I noticed something shiny in Seizō's hand.

'What about it? Why won't you tell me?'

As he said this he was holding his hand close to her cheek and I got a clear glimpse of a blade. At the same time I heard a voice that seemed to be Michiko's, saying, 'Ah! That hurts!' At the sound of her quiet yet still forceful voice I kicked aside the *shōji* and rushed into the room. Its occupants were obviously surprised.

When I entered the room, yelling, 'What are you doing?', Seizō stood up and screamed. 'What's this? Who is that?'

I seem to have collided with the mosquito net as I came in and ripped out its hooks but Seizō and I kicked it aside, after which we stood glaring at each other while Michiko lay all trussed up on the floor. The silence was deafening. Seizō had recovered from his initial shock and stood there staring at me with the knife blade still in his right hand.

It was at this moment that my descent to hell began. As that bizarre silence was broken the lives of the three people in that room were cursed forever.

It was Michiko who broke the silence.

'Ichirō-san, what a silly boy you are! Such a silly boy! Tee hee!'

When this freakish sentence came out of Michiko's mouth as she lay there with both hands tied, my world was turned upside down. Oh! Those words! That laugh!

Something flashed on in my mind and I stood there like a stone having been struck by lightning.

I could feel my brains sloshing inside my head and I began to kick the floor in frustration.

As I sit here in prison now I am struggling to remember the scene in as much detail as possible.

I experienced so many emotions at that moment that I would have been hard pressed to explain how I felt at the time, but now that I think back on it more calmly the facts all present themselves quite clearly.

Michiko's words made it all too clear.

How could I have been so foolish not to have realised it before? Seizō and Michiko did not have a normal sex life. What they were doing here was nothing less than a perverted sex game. It was true that Seizō disliked me but the two needed a good story for the perverse plays they liked to stage. At some point my name had come to play a key role in their little theatricals. The husband got his thrills from putting on a play in which he tortured his wife in order to force her to confess, while she took pleasure in being tortured.

I fell to my knees, awash in shame.

But those words of Michiko's that had already turned my world upside down were the cause of an even greater tragedy.

It was clear now that Seizō had been using me as a prop to satisfy his own desires. But did this mean that he did not actually suspect anything between Michiko and me?

In fact he did suspect us, as became clear at that moment.

Consider – while Michiko laughed off my sudden appearance on the scene, how did Seizō interpret it?

He ignored the kneeling intruder and went straight to Michiko, sidled up to her and asked, with uneven breath, 'Why is Ōtera here?'

Seizō was clearly excited by his own lines in the play he was staging. 'Couldn't this play be real? What if Michiko really did love Ōtera and was thereby satisfying a double masochism?' This is no doubt what Seizō was thinking. Indeed, the earnestness of his manner at the time suggested that he had already begun to believe it.

Seeing that Michiko remained silent he repeated himself.

'Listen you slut! You're fucking Ōtera aren't you!'

If Michiko had been able to see how serious Seizō was when he said this, the tragedy that followed might not have happened.

But Michiko wasn't paying attention.

She answered him with the same saucy tone that she always used in their games.

'Why yes! Maybe I am!'

The look on Seizō's face when he heard this surpasses description.

In the next instant something terrifying happened.

There was a sudden explosive cry of anger and distress. I started and tried to stop him but he had already stabbed Michiko in her right breast. Realising for the first time the seriousness of the situation, Michiko began to scream and to writhe in pain. Before I even had time to yell out, 'You devil!' or to reach out to stop him, he was already stabbing her again above the heart. When I tried to interfere he came after me, looking every bit like a devil, but then suddenly began to stab himself painfully in the chest. He crumpled to the floor onto his own futon, let out a groan of pain along with a mouthful of blood, and slumped forwards. I tried to help by holding his back but he only spit curses and blood at me and I saw that as he had leaned over with the knife it had somehow stuck him in the chest and now blood was rushing from his right breast and the knife was all tangled in his kimono.

I had lost all judgment. I didn't care any more what happened to me. I took the knife out of Seizō and pushed him over (this is when he hit his head on the table and injured himself). I had decided to kill myself with his knife.

But at that moment the three from downstairs came into the room and I hesitated. It was after that when I clearly heard both Seizō and Michiko say my name.

Hearing this I realised I could not die without saying anything. I had to take revenge against this woman for toying with me and against this man for having so readily concluded I was guilty of the base crime of adultery. I figured I would soon die in any case. So I calmly allowed myself to be arrested.

The preceding is the truth about what happened that night.

VIII

I had decided to have my revenge. Michiko had made me into a pawn in their game. She had told me her husband didn't love her and that he was abusing her. She had even shown me the scars! What a devil! I had felt real sympathy for her. But it was all a ruse and a lie! I was only one of many young men whom Michiko was using in this way. Sure, Michiko, you stayed faithful to your husband all right. But how many men's hearts did you trifle with in the process? Did you think this could be forgiven?

When I go to hell you're coming with me.

My dishonour in being sentenced to death is of course enormous, but it is surely no honour for *you* either to be known for having committed adultery and getting yourself killed out of blind passion. Nor does it do you any credit that your husband, who cursed me until he died, is known as a cuckold and a murder victim. Look at the two of you! Once so well regarded in society. And now you've gone and destroyed each other's reputation. This young man from the country couldn't feel less sympathy for you.

Once I was arrested I didn't say a word for an entire day while I figured out what my story would be. I thought about it for a long time and decided to take my revenge against the Odas and against the legal system at the same time.

And what was the result? That judge with the difficult look on his face wrote in the official public documents that his reason for giving me the death penalty had to do with the fact that I was involved in a long-term adulterous relationship with Michiko. Right there, in the judge's decision, was the proof that Michiko was mine forever.

The story that I dreamed up in the police office – a story that emerged from the soul of a devil – was now confirmed as a fact by the court.

Michiko's beautiful flesh was mine now.

In exchange they're going to take my useless life. What a bargain that is!

All of you who are tired of living – why not sell your souls to the devil? Turn your lives into something valuable! If you do you'll find that nothing is impossible.

Justice! How many times has blood been spilled in your name?

And you, lawyers! You have the choice to believe what I've written here or not. If you believe it you will have to admit how feeble your powers are. You might have fallen straight into my trap – but the fact is that you have put an innocent man to death. You should be ashamed of yourselves. If you don't believe what I've written, this will suit me just as well. In that case you have used the law to besmirch the reputation of a defenceless dead woman with the brand, much worse than death, of adultery. Ha! You make me laugh!

Oh Michiko! My beloved Michiko!

You are mine. You are my love.

Michiko! And yet...

Were you really sad after all? Wasn't it true that Seizō didn't love you? You might have been well matched physically and sexually, but weren't you still alone? Didn't you tell me that you were?

If that was the case, my revenge here has been all too cruel...

Michiko! Didn't you really love me? Tell me! Tell me! I am going to die.

Oh! That's right! You called my name. 'Ichirō,' you said. I know you weren't calling out to me. But did you think that I wouldn't hear this last word uttered by the woman I loved?

I know Michiko. You told the truth then. When Seizō said, 'Ōtera, Ōtera...' you heard it and used your last ounce of energy to say, 'No... It wasn't Ichirō...'

I heard it. I heard it. I was listening with my whole body to the last words of the woman I loved.

The others missed the rest of it. All they heard was my name like they were used to hearing it on your lips.

So you loved me after all. If that was true… if that was true…

Come Devil! Take me in your wings. Suck out the last human blood in my veins!

I hate women. I hate Michiko. Michiko was loyal to her husband. She never loved me. Devil! Tear my soul from my body and keep me by your side always.

Michiko. Even Michiko said my name when she died. What a hateful pair they were. Damn them both.

The law be damned!

Woman be damned!

And yet in the end I wonder… What if?…

Could Michiko have possibly –

IX

The bizarre manuscript ends here. Ōtera called out to the devil but it seems he was a human being after all. He seems to have been unable to continue since the text cuts off in midsentence. The paper is stained here and there with tears.

I will refrain from commenting on the manuscript and leave the rest for you to hypothesise and imagine. Are we to believe these earnest words? Should we simply lay them to rest as the preposterous ravings of a mad man? I will not say much.

There is one thing, however, that this unfortunate young man was no doubt wondering until the moment of his death. He wanted to know if Michiko was in fact lonely and really loved Ōtera Ichirō, or whether she got on well with her husband and was merely toying with Ōtera.

As for Michiko, it was also possible that she loved neither her husband nor Ōtera and was toying with both of them.

It is often the case with sex perverts that they are masochists on the physical level but the reverse in terms of their mentality.

It is not hard to imagine that, having been forced into a marriage for financial reasons, she allowed her husband to dominate her physically while mentally she placed herself in the opposite position.

In this case, she would have believed in her mind that she was manipulating her husband while also making a plaything out of Ōtera – thus having her fun with both men.

If that was in fact the case she managed to lose her life to the flames of jealousy that she herself had fanned in her husband.

But Ōtera was too pure a young man to imagine such a complicated situation.

He could only imagine two alternatives: either Michiko truly loved her husband or she secretly loved him. Of course this was perfectly understandable on his part.

In any case, I pray that the victims of this tragedy may rest in peace.

My prayers are always with this beautiful young man who may have perished for a crime he did not commit. And as for Michiko, who lies in the earth burdened with a vile name she may not have deserved, I make sure that there are always flowers on her grave.

Glossary

Chow: In mahjong, a set of three tiles of the same suit and consecutive numbers.

Daimyo: Hereditary rulers of the several hundred small principalities that made up feudal Japan until the dismantling of the Tokugawa Shogunate in 1868.

Obi: Kimono sash

Shōji: A sliding door made with paper glued to a wooden latticework.

Paar: The German word for 'couple' often used in pre-war Japan to refer to a male-male couple.

Tatami: Rectangular straw mats used for flooring in traditional Japanese houses. They are made in a uniform size (although the precise measurements differ by region) so the number of mats may be used to indicate the size of a room.

Biographical note

Viscount Hamao Shirō (1896–1935) was the scion of one of modern Japan's most prestigious families, a public prosecutor and a member of Japan's House of Peers. In 1928 he gave up his career as a prosecutor to devote himself to writing detective fiction. He made his debut in the following year, with 'Did He Kill Them?' in the journal *Shinseinen*, or *New Youth*, a wildly popular literary magazine that promoted the heady brew of aestheticised decadence, gothic horror and pseudo-scientific sexology and criminology known in 1920s Japan as *ero-guro-nansensu*, or 'erotic grotesque nonsense'. By his death six years later at the age of forty he had published sixteen novellas and three full-length novels, and was working on one more.

Hamao is known in the history of Japanese detective fiction for his focus on the limits of justice under the modern legal system. His shorter works tended to focus on the psychological motives behind the crime rather than the puzzle of 'whodunnit?' and often used themes of perverse sexuality to illustrate the blind spots of the law. Hamao was extremely tall and 'thin as a crane' according to his friend and fellow writer Yokomizo Seishi, but despite his imposing appearance and intimidating social position, surprisingly approachable and 'friendly enough to cure my shyness'.

HESPERUS PRESS

Hesperus Press is committed to bringing near what is far –
far both in space and time. Works written by the greatest
authors, and unjustly neglected or simply little known in
the English-speaking world, are made accessible through
new translations and a completely fresh editorial approach.
Through these classic works, the reader is introduced to the
greatest writers from all times and all cultures.

For more information on Hesperus Press, please visit our
website: **www.hesperuspress.com**